I MADE MY BOY OUT OF POETRY

Authors Choice Press
San Jose New York Lincoln Shanghai

I Made My Boy Out of Poetry

Authors Choice Press
an imprint of iUniverse.com, Inc.

For information address:
iUniverse.com, Inc.
5220 S 16th, Ste. 200
Lincoln, NE 68512
www.iuniverse.com

Originally published by Author

ISBN: 0-595-15765-3

Printed in the United States of America

I MADE
MY BOY
OUT OF
POETRY

**Poems, stories, dreams and sho 'nuff truths
by Aberjhani**

To Walker Evans --
Wishing you joy
in your literary
and other creative
pursuits --
Aberjhani
4/13/01

To Vera Annette Lloyd Trappio
Whose love refused to fail

Acknowledgements

Respect to the following: My Savannah posse: The Savannah Writers Group, The Poetry Society of Georgia, all former Blue House Center for Creativity Affiliates, and the Receding Wave/Open Mic Show; my Big Brother Wallace for keeping me in motion; my Sufi Brother Showgi who brought balm to Gilead; my family for passing on to me the gift and passion for sharing stories; the good brother Nadra Enzi for sharing knowledge and inspiration; Lara Ramaswamy and Cedric Stratton for sharing their formidable brain power; and computer hero extraordinaire Kevin Phillips for pushing me across the finish line.

Mad props also to my Brother in Creativity Luther E. Vann, whose spiritually-realized art gave the following poems their titles: "In A Quiet Place on A Quiet Street"; "Family Reunion: Remembering the Ancestors"; "The Light, That Never Dies"; "Washington Park No. 162"; "Past Present and Future Are One"; and "For the Love of the Poet".

Gratitude to the following publications in which some of this book's material first appeared: THE AFRICAN-AMERICAN LITERARY REVIEW; THE SAVANNAH LITERARY JOURNAL; POETS, ARTISTS & MADMEN; THE DULL FLY; OUT OF THE BLUE; THE SAVANNAH TRIBUNE; THE GEORGIA GUARDIAN; THE ANGRY FIXX.

Table of Contents

Section One: Fiction

Section Two: Poetry

Section Three: Fiction

Section Four: Poetry

Section Five: Fiction

Section Six: Poetry

Section Seven: Fiction

Section Eight: Poetry

Section Nine: Fiction

Section Ten: Poetry

Section Eleven: Essay

"I was born by the river
in a little tent
and just like that river
I've been running ever since..."
   Sam Cooke
   (A Change Is Gonna Come)

"I do not offer the old smooth prizes,
but offer rough new prizes..."
   Walt Whitman
   (Song of the Open Road)

Elijah's Skin

"In me is His theater of manifesta-
tion..."
Ibn Al-Arabi
(Seals of Wisdom)

For fifteen years Elijah had been traveling then one night went
to sleep beside the railroad tracks across from the Heavenly
Daze housing project. Dreams rose up in him like a hot
swamp steamy with grief, or a cold knife slash dragging from
the middle of his groin to the top of his throat. His right arm
rested meekly on the metal rail like Isaac waiting for death at
his own father's holy hand and he dreamed of his lovely dead
wife and his soft dead son without envisioning anything at all.

The vibrations he felt in his sleep had nothing to do with
his soul easing out of his body as he dreamily thought; they
came solely from the weight and motion of the freight train
rolling north to deliver fuel, furniture and other items having
no relevance to Elijah's life or his dreaming. On the metal rail
his arm itched like a nose with a feeling that something bad
was about to happen. In another life the sound of the train
would have been reminiscent of certain songs by Muddy
Waters or even Bruce Springsteen but not in this one. In this
life the sound stabbed viciously against the night exactly like a
human being demonstrating flawless disrespect for the life of
another human being.

As the huge train steamed closer toward the not-as-huge
arm propped across the rail, Elijah smiled in the middle of his
dream and decided it was time to kiss. When his front tooth
broke on a large rock, he opened his eyes and shaped his
mouth to curse. His reflexes took over and he screamed
instead. His body jerked away from the track and the freight

1

train roared past him like a giant blind beast with no manners at all.

He jumped to his feet with the swiftness and coordination that are possible only when one's entire body responds to a single thought even before it forms itself. The danger having passed, he no longer considered it.

Where was he? He looked across the street at the Heavenly Daze Project. Years ago --how many? fortyfive? thirtyeight? twentynine?-- he had been born in one of those apartments when his mother thought she needed to use the bathroom but instead wound up giving birth to him. Since then, he had been a lot of things: soldier, poet, thief, magician. Probably too many things. He crossed the street and entered the project, realizing he had come back for something, yet possessing neither a memory nor a sense of what it might be.

When he passed the row of block apartments facing the street he'd just crossed, Elijah entered a courtyard of several rectangular buildings and came upon three young men kicking, slapping and generally abusing a fourth man curled into a ball on the ground. As he walked closer to them, one young man immediately turned away from his attack and approached Elijah with a smile of deep concern. He put an arm around Elijah's waist --though Elijah was much taller-- called him "Brother," and asked if he were "alright."

"No, um, I don't think so."

"Yeah Brother you look troubled but I can help you, I got what you need man, check this out." The man pulled Elijah so close that their bodies increased each other's heat. He held up a hand full of pills and little white stones that Elijah recognized but did not want. When Elijah touched the man's face, he saw that he was more boy than man. A manboy: possibly the age his son would have been by now. He turned away and went to the two men beating on another. They were so surprised when he lifted the beaten man away from them and stood him on his feet that for several seconds they kicked and pounded the dirt before realizing the man was no longer there.

The manboy with the deep concern turned to him and said: "Brother I tried to help you and look what chu doin, why you doin that, this man owe me money and obviously he gotta pay."

"He's hurt. Shouldn't you leave him alone?"

The three men laughed. One of them lifted a knife, slashed it across Elijah's chest and ripped his shirt completely from his torso. Then their mouths dropped slowly open and someone

2

said "damn!" as they looked at Elijah's skin: his hands, arms, back, sides, chest and belly were covered with scars, some of them shaped like ragged rivers, others like crescent moons, and still others like the letters of a new alphabet. The darkness of its hue seemed almost an exact duplicate of the blackness of the night. Light reflecting from street lamps and porch lights gleamed upon his skin like stars and diamonds converging in a private universe trying hard to give birth to itself. One of the young men looked at it and vomited. A second stared until he became dizzy and thought he was falling through a vortex of shadows and burning ice. The manboy with deep concern angrily spat blood on Elijah's chest. And the man who'd been beaten into the dirt blinked dry tears against the frozen air.

When the deeply concerned manboy raised his knife to stab him, Elijah pointed beneath the right side of his chest and suggested that would be the best place to strike; truly it was the one place not already occupied by a scar.

"You crazy man, get the hell away from us!" But they ran before Elijah could think to do so. Then he turned towards the beaten man to ask him about families he once knew in the project, but he had also run away.

The Old Woman, he thought, she can help me. Is she still alive? For some reason he knew the answer was yes, even though the woman had been considered very old when he was born and must now be an age when most people would be in their graves. Or in heaven. Or in hell. Or just bumming around Earth minus their physical bodies.

As he walked through the project searching for the Old Woman he allowed surprise to open his eyes. It was neither the opprobrious presence of boarded up doors and windows signalling mass exodus from Heavenly Daze nor the ease with which people offered him pleasure or violence that astonished him. It was the sudden awareness of how small everything was. The second-story porches from which he had jumped as a child had seemed back then as if they were thirty feet above the ground; now it was clear they were barely nine. And the apartments themselves were so impersonally miniature that it seemed ludicrous to believe they contained entire histories of individual ecstasies and apocryphal miseries.

He learned from several different people that numerous men he had known were in jail, or dead, or living under conditions equivalent to both. He learned while speaking with oth-

3

ers that words and phrases considered profane when he lived there were now accepted as standard forms of expression. Then he found the Old Woman.

She sat in the doorway of her ground-level apartment on the same street where he had been born. Another man would have wondered why she sat in an open doorway on a cold night within a neighborhood where few people had fewer than three locks on each door and iron bars on every window. Elijah didn't. She had been when he was born and was now as then a large woman, a pipe-smoker. The power of her frame, like the ancient color of her face, and the thunderous quiet lighting her eyes created the illusion she was not sitting in a wheelchair. He told her his name and asked if she remembered him.

"Boy I know who you is better den you do. Who you think pulled your mama's silly ass off that toilet when you was being born and saved your life?"

These words made Elijah sad because she'd spoken them with love and he knew they were true. He told her that he had been hurt. "Something happened to me. I've been hurt real bad. I...uh...I think I got damaged."

She leaned forward: "Course you been hurt. You was born to hurt. What make you wanna forget somethin that important? Power that's worth somethin --real power!--live an' grow from the hurt you feed it."

"Then where's mine? That power you're talkin about? Is it the kind that can...give a man back his life? I don't...I think I got damaged..."

She reached out and pinched a single thick line of skin, scar tissue as pronounced as the dry flames crackling in his voice, zigzagging from one mound of his chest to the other. She then ran one broad, heated hand from the bottom of his throat down to his waist, pressing against the broken ridges of scars as if releasing from them meanings he had never known they possessed. His breath drew sharply in and vertigo arched suddenly from the moon to his skull; his heart snagged between one impulse to scream and another to laugh. He heard the woman's voice:

"You think destiny your enemy. It ain't boy. Destiny your power."

From the edge of a cliff inside himself he fell a thousand feet. Hitting bottom felt so much like rapture that his scream split the night in half. When Elijah woke up, he was sitting in the old woman's wheelchair, the sunrise bleeding pale gold and

4

white against the sky. Slowly he stood, looked around. The Old Woman's gone. When he returned to the doorway, he found a boy nine or ten and a young woman with a pained face holding a very large stomach. Sunlight blazed around them as if it believed itself an angel. The boy said the young woman was his sister and they needed the Old Woman's help, very quickly, to deliver her baby.

"She's gone," said Elijah.

They asked what they should do. Elijah looked first at his scarred hands, then at the young woman's trembling legs stained with fluid. He placed one troubled finger upon her face covered over with terror. He had been so many things: soldier, poet, thief, magician. Probably too many things.

Divine Morphology

Yesterday my heart was an onion.
Your love swerving east like an ax
chopped it in half
and sucked tears from the breasts
of a pregnant summer sky.

This morning my heart became a candied yam.
All mixed up with a thousand secret spices
I had no taste for praising or condemning.
I steamed, smouldered and burned
with every kiss that glistened inside your eyes.

Tomorrow,
or three seconds from now,
I shall become something else,

such as that silent white glow
in the air between your lips
when your soul breaks open like a fresh galaxy
and releases the buried typhoon of your fears;

or a leaf that flashes jade
for a season
then folds back into the topaz mysteries
gathered inside autumn's tattered pocket.
Before this song comes to an end
my heart shall beat and surface
through many images:
a groom, a bride, the ring on each of their fingers.
The vows that make their tongues sweet.

One infinite flux of beauty--
like that one just now--
and my heart becomes your ears
lovingly swallowing these words,
buzzing like a star gone wild.
Getting hot. Now hotter. Like raw honey catching fire.

Calligraphy of Intimacy

Perhaps one day our togetherness
will resemble the calligraphic design
of the letters that spell Abd Al-Jami,
a name denoting beauty: both inside and out.

Like the Arabic character alif
curving its loveliness towards
the end of a numinous breath
you will wander towards an unseen mountain,
re-emerging into life by way of bazaars
in Morocco. Or cafes in Paris.
While I nurse sand dunes and canyons,
shaking with the delicious certainty
that your wanderings and mine
will soon converge, and lock, in the hair
and screaming of the same urgent fire.

Like the seductive lines and silences
of Islamic calligraphy we will bow
and clash three thousand swords.
Or disappear between the warm shadows
of hands, whispers and kissing
disguised and protected by the shields of art.

Out of the canvas of our passion confusion
will rise up, blinding those too curious
about who we are. Or what we do.
Beauty will snatch us by the heart
and love us until we are raw with understanding.
Like two well-paid royal scribes we will let our
hands explain each other to each other and learn
at last to comprehend this calligraphy called intimacy.

Remembrance of a River Past

Back when I was Nile
ancient dawn speaking reflections
of God's hidden hunger I would flow
quietly sometimes, lacing amber and blue
between the panther black of your somber lashes
sometimes like a shimmering stream
of moon-colored goddesses or the milk-white tears
of an abused virtue, I would flow
out of my chest towards and all around you
as though a shower of glittering singers
sometimes this is how it was when you would stand
vulva-deep in the center of my melting eyes
and I sometimes would thirst then drink
regaining lost knowledge of heaven & self
I would splash my colors innocent
upon your belly and fingers and lips
cloaking your thighs like a vineyard of liquid leaves
rock the cradle and smoke the legend
of your sphinx-woman gaze, just sweet
as any river might please, to claim you
sometimes, in those dawns spoken ancient
and ancient ago, when the beauty of thee
was all the beauty, a river need know

The Vision of Roses

I dreamed that I was standing outside at night in a garden with Oprah Winfrey. I have my arms around her waist as I ask about her day. She murmurs an inconsequential response when I look up and notice the sky between the branches of the trees. As I stare at the sky, I suddenly see millions of red and purple roses flowing out of the full moon. The roses then change into a cluster of berries that fill the sky with sheer beauty. Suddenly I find myself overwhelmed by the splendor of the vision and I fall to the ground trying to catch my breath. I tell Oprah that all this beauty is overwhelming me. I hold onto a fence as I pull myself to my feet, staring at the moon as it turns into a giant rose and fills the sky with millions of shining flowers and berries.

Then my dream changes completely and I find myself sitting at a desk preparing to write something. As soon as I start to write, I remember the dream I just had. I physically wake up from this second dream, grab my notebook and write down as much as I can recall.

Blood and Blossoms

Unless you are here: this garden refuses to exist.
Pink dragonflies fall from the air
and become scorpions scratching blood out of rocks.
The rainbows that dangle upon this mist: shatter.
Like the smile of a child separated
from his mother's milk for the very first time.

But with my arms circling your breasts
and my lips at home upon your ears:
the universe opens one gate after another
and we step into gestures made of pure sanctity and grace.

Our first journey here we found only a road
made of ice and dust. Do you recall the breeze
that stripped us naked and twirled upon its
finger a single bright petal? I remember tumbling
like a silk feather through your heart
then dropping to my knees and staring up at the moon.

Staring up at the moon. I saw his silver mouth
slowly open. My heart clenched with terror
as a wide stream of blood suddenly gushed
beneath the stars and came spilling towards Earth.
Horror chewed our bones into wax as wave
after wave of brilliant crimson rushed down the sky
and we prepared to drown in a monsoon of blood.

How much time would there be: to scorn death and love you?
Would escape prove possible through your eyes or mine?

Whereas fear had made the night into a slave
suddenly it was liberated by a vision of bliss.
A rose blossom scorched my cheek with a whisper.
When we again looked into the sky, the crimson waves
we had taken for blood had moved closer
and we could see that they were not blood at all.

Flowing out of the moon's mouth in the shape
of a long trailing spiral were countless red roses.
Roses as red as an evening sun or a mountain covered with
     rubies.
For every blossom that fell the earth would moan
and a nightingale spring singing from its grave
or a tiny blue star would shiver white ecstasy.

I dared to rise and hold you with hands
that were filled with somebody's tears
as roses came whirling out of the jubilant dark
and carnelian starlight turned our very skin
into rising waves of soul-hot pleasure.
Each time our lips touched our lungs filled
with the scent of honey and eternal mystery.

All of Eden was reborn and forgiven
as we opened like mystical pathways
and fed the earth with nectar from our laughing hearts.
We were so sticky with joy that we lost our humanity.
That was the only moment I have ever prayed would last
     forever.
And that is the only moment which ever has.

Unless you are here: this garden refuses to exist.

The Language My Body Speaks

If my lips should flutter and cuddle
next to yours, like a butterfly
matching its colors
with the dewy-morning splendor of hyacinth--
do not think I am only trying to steal a kiss.

Or if my arms suddenly circle your waist
like silver surrounding a virgin moon,
and my belly trembles heated signals of smoke
all up and down the burning shores of your flesh--
do not think I desire scandal, or infamy.

There is a reason that my voice huddles
like a child made of broken wings inside your heart.

The language my body speaks is less eloquent
than French, and not so precise as Swahili.
Sometimes my shoulders are speaking to you
of how I was raped at the age of twelve.
Sometimes my kiss is humming the poetry
that pulled the gun out of my mouth.

A wise African named Nadra told me the language
of angels is what makes the earth spin,
and what causes the sun to shine drunk with love.
Perhaps I shall learn a word or two.
Maybe then, you will understand?

The One Heart

Did you remember to make one heart
soft, wretched, and bold enough to love mine?
In what country is it dreaming
and at what hour should I whisper its name?
Has it been blessed
with the lovely cruel eyes of a baby seal,
or cursed with the all-consuming vision
of some god such as Odin?

Did you make one heart beautiful,
scarred, and starved enough to come find me?
Like a rich king's castle it will need
more chambers than usual:
   one where flutes and guitars may share their love-play,
   another where we can each forget the other exists,
   and yet another where we may flood each other with light
   and longing and fire until we are insane with our throbbing.

Did you hide it inside a body muscled with music
or within some ancient soul covered over
with the kneeling green of a weeping willow?
I should like, I think, for its kiss
to taste like roses. And I recall
from a glorious dream that its hair
should smell like the sea.

Did you remember to make one heart to love mine?
Did you make each ounce of blood
from the perfume of a pure and perfect patience?
Did you build each trembling wall out of compassion
strong enough to hold a man so unlovely and foolish as I?

Did you remember to make one heart
soft, wretched, and bold enough to claim my heart?
In what country is it dreaming
and at what hour should I whisper its name?
Does it know where my sorrow lives
and has anyone shown it where our bliss is waiting?

And you —You— will you forgive me for not remembering
that yours is a love which never forgets.

Strange River

These waters are strange: loping
like a crippled galaxy through the nightmares
flowing freely through your heart,
and worse, my love, they are the only
part of you I can still touch.

Once I could glide
through the silvery depths
of your good and evil
and let myself float, or drown,
or bubble back to life,
breathing naked upon the shores of your kindness
while the light of our evening bliss
covered me like a forest
and forced my fear to remake itself
into some lonely god's image.

Now: these waters are polluted.
And in all fairness I recognize
the globs of shit that I dumped here,
and I can smell the ashes of infidelities
that erupted out of you in response.
Standing in the flow of your quivering rhythms
pieces of metal slash my thighs
and dead shark fall crying against my chest.

I drop beneath the waves of our past, feeling
for the heated throb and echo of forgotten undercurrents.
Something delicious swallows my entire body
and sucks dry the bones of my sentimentality.

I watch your tides recede into damaged obscurity.
Upon the shores of your abandoned heart
I am a fisherman, dangling worms, where nothing bites.

In A Quiet Place On A Quiet Street

In a quiet place on a quiet street
where no one will ever find us
we sit with souls curled around each other
watching connections and mysteries
braid themselves together
like prophecies past and future
bringing enlightenment to the present.

The architecture of personal fate
and public destiny
reflect a fine and mellow logic
easily comprehensible
to the heart's magnificent genius,
but often unfathomable
to intellect's limited vision.

Silence brings us new names
new feelings and new knowledge.
Dreams dress us carefully
in the colors of power and faith.
In this quiet place on a quiet street
where no one ever finds us
gently, lovingly, freedom gives back our pain.

In Minutes When

In minutes when
the stars
seduce
the sun
we will run naked
between
bayonet trees
and corporate daggers,
and we will dive
into the lake
of whispering dawns
where our first touch
will be a new star
in the universe
and our second touch
will be nova.

Koo 12

The moon is a window inside
the house of the sun.
Beneath its pale lovely tears
I envision your belly as
bronze-colored poetry,
our every candy-sticky sigh
a liquid metaphor describing fire.

Company For Melissa

"Everybody thinks of the noise and
the power of you. But I have heard
and felt the softness."
Anais Nin
(Henry and June)

Is someone at the door? Oh my, just a moment please, don't
go anywhere, I'll be right there. Just let me open this nasty old
lock and... there! Oh, what a lovely surprise indeed. Too many
years have passed since a handsome young man made it his
business to knock on my door, but please forgive my chatter
and fuss and come inside, come inside, so lovely to have you
here. Please have a seat Mr.....Ahhh, Mr. Hollynut. I have
been widowed more than once so I have several names but the
one which I'm most fond of is my own: Melissa. And would you
by any chance be of relation to the Hollynuts in Boston? No?
Well I didn't think so actually but I thought perhaps I saw a
faint resemblance about the eyes and the cheeks there.
Imagine such an audacious old woman like myself daring to
trust her vision at my age, but enough of my prattle Mr.
Hollynut, it's only that I am truly moved that you have come to
visit me. Most people simply don't bother leaving the highway
and risking their fine cars on the dirt road leading to my home
you see, and what is that you have there, those papers in your
attaché case? Ahhh, I see, magazines, and what fine maga-
zines they appear to be Mr. Hollynut, such colorful pictures on
the covers. Yes, fine indeed. So am I to assume my friend that
you are a magazine salesman? No? Then may I inquire... Oh,
you are one of Heaven's Elite, a religious group, yes yes, I have
seen your members strolling about the parks in town offering
fellowship and enlightenment to the citizens of our fair com-

munity. You are a commendable organization of people doing commendable work. I applaud you, oh I do indeed. Hmmmm? You'd like to discuss the magazines and the Bible with me? Why how thoughtful of you Mr. Hollynut, yes, what a lovely idea was that!. Ha ha hee hee, oh my, I'm feeling giddy all over, you are taking me back to years when I performed upon the stage and a playwright I knew had me utter the words, "How lovelyish yonder inspiration that shines 'pon thy brow like glorious Venus upon the heart of all love." Is that not "lovelyish" indeed Mr. Hollynut? Truly it is, even as the sweet brown contours of your face are lovelyish, even as the flowing firmness of all which makes you a man Mr. Hollynut but I have digressed, haven't I my friend? But fear not, for nothing has been sullied. And as it happens, I know the perfect way for us to return to our original course: you shall read aloud to me from your wonderful magazines while I make us some tea. Those of your persuasion are allowed tea, are they not? Very good, yes, very good truly. Just continue reading and I shall have no problem hearing you while in the kitchen. My eyes have withered as things of great beauty are known to do but my hearing remains keen. I think you will like this tea. It is of an African blend not often found in this corner of our dear little planet.

Did I hear you scream Mr. Hollynut? Oh yes, you will find that the mice are plentiful in my home. When I was a younger woman, in my eighties or so I would drive them away with poisons and traps but as my age progressed and visits and messages from those who once loved me became less frequent, I began to find the mice and other little friends around the house quite a comfort. Once I looked in the mirror and saw that a little white one had attached himself to my hair and I must confess that at first I was somewhat vexed, then I realized that he looked much like a white rose sitting there, so I let him remain for a time and we got on quite well. But please do continue reading, our tea is ready now and I shall bring it inside.

You were telling me something about the lessons of faith and righteousness as demonstrated in the Old Testament by the stories of David and Saul. I put honey in the tea, I hope you'll like it. Now, let us sit and talk of things beautiful, wise and holy. Though I tend to be more partial to the New Testament, I must say that the story of David is one of my favorites and I've always found his friendship with Jonathan --now he was Solomon's son, wasn't he? No, he was Saul's-- I

18

always thought their friendship to be the stuff of which the most divine poems are written, absolutely inspired and absolutely inspiring. In the part of the story where they are in the meadow, kissing each other goodbye, my heart broke for them Mr. Hollynut. It broke as cleanly and completely as it did when I played Linda in Mr. Miller's *Death of A Salesman* in London. It doesn't shame me to say I wept twice as hard for she who had buried the dreamer as I did for he who had dreamed. My tears for the stage came easily that season Mr. Hollynut for they were the same tears which I refused to shed when a promise of marriage was broken as callously as a twig off a bush. And the man who did it was the same actor who played my husband Willy and I would tell you his name Mr. Hollynut but you would know him too well, he may even have been a hero to you when you were a boy and I would not wish to tarnish your memory of him. He is a ghost who sits weeping in this dusty castle of my heart, reciting soliloquies of things that should have been. But I have digressed again, haven't I? Forgive an old woman her memories of youth Mr. Hollynut. We were speaking of David and Jonathan and their wonderful friendship.

That friends who shared a covenant should have been forced into the role of enemies is pure tragedy Mr. Hollynut, for was it not said that they 'loved one another with a love surpassing that of women.' Yes, it was said just so and I had friends, dear friends in the theater, who took that to mean that David and Jonathan were lovers as well as friends. What is your view on the possibility of such a reality Mr. Hollynut? 'Abominable'? Oh. Then you do surprise me, yes, you do indeed, for I would have felt such a bonding of heart and soul and flesh to be mightier than one of steel chains or velvet handcuffs Mr. Hollynut. I would have equated such a bonding with love in its purest form but I'm an old woman who spent many of her years in theater and many others pretending to be a novelist of some merit and all of that was so long ago that my views of life on the planet are bound to collide with some of the truths which a young man like yourself may have discovered in the modern world.

Oh dear! Is it my words that have caused you to choke or is your tea too strong? Most likely I should have warned you that it is quite powerful, an African blend of certain leaves and roots called yohije. There are tribes in the continent's deeper interior who mix the tea with elderly gentlemen's, er, 'seed,'

19

and drink it during rites of fertility but you need not fear Mr. Hollynut, it has been a very long time since I had access to such a precious ingredient and we are oceans away from Africa's mysterious bosom, are we not? I've even been told that some people roll the tea into cigarettes and smoke them but I can't imagine the value of such a practice.

My but you are flushed Mr. Hollynut! It is the tea, isn't it? Well the best remedy is to drink even more of it so that you come to master its effect, you see. My apologies for making it so strong, though I did say I rarely brewed this particular blend and I suppose I've grown accustomed to it over the years myself. Do not worry, you shall be fine. Here, let me help you out of that stuffy jacket and loosen your tie so you can breathe better. See, the color is coming back to your face already, and what a lovelyish face it is Mr. Hollynut, such a full warm friendly mouth, such a handsome girlish pair of eyes with lashes like that. Here my dear, sip your tea, and sip some more. Yes, yes.

Now let us continue to read from your very fine magazines and do not mind me if I mutter and ramble a bit to myself as you are reading for it means only that I find your voice stimulating, pretty, caressing. Hmmm, yes, yes.

Did I hear you use the word spiritualism? Would that be a bad or good thing in your devout estimation? A bad thing? Hmmm, I am inclined, perhaps, to agree with you because I recall when the spirit of my second husband used to come to the house in the middle of the night, ranting and raving about a man with whom he thought I'd been unfaithful while he was alive. Oh he would yell and stomp his feet for hours, accusing me of sleeping with Terrence Daniels, which I had done of course but he really had no way of knowing that and I don't believe that was truly Earnest's spirit anyway becau-- What's that? A demon you say? Oh no dear boy, it was no demon; I'm not afraid to put those creatures in their place. This was actually some kind of off-shoot of Earnest's personality --if you will follow my meaning-- a part of him which knew by instinct that I truly had shared my charms with another, a man so beautiful that a woman would have to have been comatose within a steel body cast to keep her hands off him. He was the only time I dallied outside any of my three marriages Mr. Hollynut. He was the only man worth such a transgression and I pray that many a woman got her share of him. The memory of our single rendezvous, down by the lake in-- Well, I shall

save us both from embarrassment at the memory of that love-
lyish event, that flowerglorious time in my mid-youth.

If Earnest had been a woman, or a certain kind of man, he
would have understood, but he was a man with a delicate ego
and so some portion of him would come to visit me from time
to time, raise nine kinds of hell then calm down and pee on the
rug. He made me very unhappy for a long time Mr. Hollynut.
You mustn't look so surprised my dear young man, these
things happen in the world. Please, drink your tea before it
gets too cold. You like it now, do you? That's good dear. Shall
I finish telling you about Earnest? Yes, of course. So it was
that he came to me often until one night while he was ranting
like every madman in New York, a tiny Angel came and hov-
ered in the air just before his face. Within her tiny eyes was the
greatest depth of compassion and love and sorrow that I have
ever witnessed one living soul express for another Mr.
Hollynut. She kneeled there in the air before him and it was
obvious she was praying but what came to my ears dear boy
was music of such tender eloquence, such divine passion and
grace that my listening to it seemed, somehow, to be a viola-
tion. Need I say that wonders such as that are not wrought of
the physical plane but of a place far finer my friend, a place far
far finer. And when the Angel stopped kneeling, the music also
ceased as the Angel looked toward the ceiling and began to
rise. She floated up wordlessly and Earnest followed her like
someone who had been retrieved from a wilderness of icy flam-
ing grief. He never came back after that but the music lingered
with me for years. The peace of it lingers still, so you see, while
I have had my problems with spirits, I have a great fondness
for Angels.

My, how joyful it is to be sitting here with a man so hand-
some and young like yourself Mr. Hollynut. I so rarely receive
visitors and solitude is not one to show much kindness. Those
who are beautiful and young rarely have time for those who are
otherwise and yet here you are. On my couch in my sitting
room. With me beside you. Imagine such a thing, such a
whim of an old woman's fancy and you with no wedding ring.
With your body looking so strong and firm Mr. Hollynut, the
body of a young bull who knows what awaits him in the pas-
ture. And yet you are of those who call themselves Elite, drink-
ing a tea grown by people who think of themselves only as men
and women. No, the room is not spinning my dear but you are
right to say it is very warm. I have no electric air you see, but

21

here, let me unbutton your shirt and help you become cooler. There is no need to struggle, I am only helping you. See? Let the cool air soothe your powerful chest and the lovely ripples of your belly. Such a strong body and you are forbidden to share it with those you know, are you not? Yes, yes. But strength in a man is like a song in a bird: it must express itself, it must come forth without such trappings as shame or fear or needless preoccupation with oneself. You look so disoriented Mr. Hollynut, and it's plain to see why. You have never allowed your strength to express itself but I can assist you dear sir, my frailty and softness the perfect compliment to your strength and hardness. I will help rid you of your confusions. Simply lie back and allow me to remove this troublesome garment, and this other one here. See how you soar and shine within my wise caress. This song that is your strength has sought all along to release itself into the sun and air of a gentle caring passion. A gentle mercy. This is why you came to me Mr. Hollynut, though you may have known it not. Yes dear boy, shake and tremble and cry, let your fire sing to mine, yes, yes, sing to Melissa Mr. Hollynut, sing! Sing! OH!

Dear gracious me, whatever have we done? We seem to have let Venus and Eros have their way with us this fine afternoon. Nevertheless, all is quite well as I can see the light of sanity returning to your eyes and like me, you are wondering how we came to let our desires treat us like slaves. There are few who can resist the full tug of the power of a new and true romance Mr. Hollynut. Few indeed.

And how you honor me now with your tears! Who would have dreamed that when you knocked upon my door so much would have come so soon. But let me adjust myself --aahhhh, sweet sweet sweet young man!-- so that you may become more comfortable. Or perhaps you would care to go upstairs where we may recline more like--

Oh there's no need to hurry and dress. Only you, I, and the mice are here and perhaps an Angel watching in secret but she will tell none of your church people. Please! Don't rush out the door, taking your fine magazines, your strength and young company. You can stay longer. You can stay as long as you... like.

Well, he must have thought he'd insulted me, or perhaps he feared that we had made a child, but if he'd just waited, I could have assured him that his fears were groundless. And we truly were having such a grand time. Doubtless his wound-

22

ed sense of chivalry shall heal and in time he will tell other young men of our brief romance today. Those who are most curious will one day knock upon my door and of course I shall let them in. It is always so wonderful when company comes. We will sit and talk of things wise and beautiful as we sip our cups of tea.

From the Life Between Living

I must'a been a man this last time around
    the ghost of pain still beats my spine

I must'a built certain fires to keep my eyes warm
    the smell of coffee shimmers roses through my soul

I think I enjoyed the wilderness that throbbed inside my hands
    there are legends about the sky laughing at my vanity

I believe I thought myself a mystic unnaturally born
    clouds of remembrance flash pyramids bowing before my
    heart

Or was I a black subspirit beneath the white-hot sun of Georgia
    so dearly I loved women but by men's evil remained fucked

I must'a tried my hand at happiness maybe once or twice
    Jesus, Muhammed, Kerouac, Buddha: try to teach me
    even now

I must'a laughed naked in somebody's naked arms
    (oh how I pray I laughed naked in somebody's naked arms)

I must'a been a man this last time around
    My brothers' voices are screaming odes to my death

I must'a been a man this last time around
my sisters' voices are stirring poison with my name

I must'a wagged a penis at one end and confusion at the
    other
the ghost of pain still beats my spine

Big Black Man Within A
Nonsociopoliticohistorical Context

Snowflakes roll calmly over the edge
of your amusement, drift down like shredded sky.
They are temporary and not serious,
placing their entire bodies upon the mouths
of the chrysanthemums and violets that fill
this field. I am a blackness, and a melody,
and a serving of the universe's curiosity
about itself, watching the snow fall
and melt upon the tongue of my bare chest,
or fly into the curly black rhapsody
of cosmic forest lush beneath my naval,
leaving diamonds and blue to kindle my riddle.

My knees are at home resting on the earth's shoulder
even as my spirit has been at home expanding
and exploring the energy and pulse of Sirius.
And a sunflower as tall as I wraps its leaves
around my waist as if it were all compassion
and nothing else. We feed each other our personal
mythologies, weeping about the power of shadows
and light over our past. A seductive aroma
strokes the melanin inside my skin and we shudder
prophecies from one moon to the next.
The soft gray hair of dusk spreads outward,
joins with the whirling dervish snow
to choreograph a jazz ballet of magnetic bliss.
There is an oak tree fond of telling the tale
of my origins and possible destinies.
There is a river singing ballads of miracles
I have yet to achieve. This lion standing in
majestic silence is an undiluted sexuality
rooted in the gardens of infinity.

Looking up from the lush tapestry of this
nightfallen moment, every third star is a lover
with whom I have found neverending
enigma and uncontainable sweetness. This snow
falling upon this hill melts down my spine as if I am
made of history and it is nothing less than revelation.
We absorb just enough of each other to discover
a thousand new ways to love and be loved.

My arms are the mountains that hold time in its place
My tears are the atoms that give substance to space.
My blackness is the music eternity makes when manifesting
as me.

Coconut Soda Hometown Remembrance

I have a coconut soda hometown remembrance,
of a blue-moon day in August, in fact it may
have been the 4th of July. I recall three horseflies
gulping red at the brand new blood creek running
from my mama's mouth down her chin to a small county
at the base of her throat. A Billie Holiday record
swinging in the living room spread her gardenia-perfumed
voice over the corner where all our neighbors could see
Mama, Daddy, Uncle Winston and Aunt Lucy settin' fire
to a buncha ghosts jumpin' out'a their hearts. My Daddy
and Uncle Winston had large pee stains on their pants
and thus Aunt Lucy declared they were "pissy drunk."

I have a coconut soda hometown remembrance
of the morning Aunt Lucy burned all the
biscuits but made us children, me and Little Big Boy
and CarrieBell, eat the charcoal-crusted bread
anyway, 'cause wasn't no mo' food in the house
except for some coconut cream sodas
Mama brought home from a party. And the biscuits
was nasty but chewin' on 'em drowned out the sound
of my daddy and Uncle Winston yelling in the front yard
'til one of their ghosts screamed so loud it scared
the ink-black burnt-up taste right out of those biscuits.

I have a coconut soda hometown remembrance
of standing in the front yard chewin' on biscuits
when my Mama stood between Daddy and Uncle Winston
'til they both slapped her at the same time and she
crumbled like an empire knocked to its mortal knees.
Uncle Winston's hazel-green eyes poured melting knives
into my Daddy's copper-colored gaze and Uncle Winston
pointed at me as he shouted: "We gotta get this thing straight
Joe-Joe! Those two youngest ones is yours and ain't nobody
disputin' that! But that oldest boy mine! Your wife know it!
You know it! And that boy got the right to know it too!
He nine years old and he got the right to know it too!"

I have a coconut soda hometown remembrance
of a blue-moon day in August, July 4th.
My Daddy and Uncle Winston arguing in the front yard.
My Mama crying, "Ain't none'a this necessary!
Y'all know this ain't necessary in front of these children."
And her voice like a scratched Billie Holiday record.
And me workin' on one of Aunt Lucy's biscuits
when the sunlight slicked its tongue against a knife
in my Daddy's hand. Then it flashed again and the knife
was in Uncle Winston's hand, and even without closing
my eyes same-strange-color-as-Uncle-Winston's eyes,
I can at this moment still see my daddy's spirit
shootin' like an arrow out'a his bones while his body
fell into Uncle Winston's arms as if he needed to kiss him.
Uncle Winston looked at me once. Once. Then he ran.

I have a coconut soda hometown remembrance
of my Aunt Lucy trying with two hands to cover
three children's eyes. My Daddy's body dropping like a bomb.
My Mama apologizing for burning Aunt Lucy's biscuits
and telling me, "Drink this soda-water baby, hurry up,
it ain't gon wash that nasty taste out your mind,
but it'll help you swallow the one in your mouth."

Family Reunion: Remembering the Ancestors

In addition to my blackness I am
allow me to say, a maker of eons,
goldsmith of kingdoms worn like diamonds
upon the flashing fingers of eternity.
Allow me please to confess that upon my
midnight-colored ways have sat the robes
of nobility, sublime and just and sacred;
the crown of genius has molded my brow
and the throne of destiny cradled my days
for unto my soul all things have spoken
and to my song all souls have danced.
Kings and thieves, poets and whores--
these and more from my garden have sprung
for mine is an orchard wherein each moment
possibility creates anew, beauty and shame alike:
a totality equal and divine before the law of itself.

In addition to my blackness I walk sometimes
where God weaves existence into creation,
where reality and I speak each other
into the pages of a truth unbound by this world.

Return to Savannah

Memories: vicious
like a thicket made hot
with cobras. The wrong step
or an erroneous beat
of the heart
and I could turn
into a tower bursting with death.

Legends tell the tourists
that spectres roam this city
but I've no need of tales
to explain
the red-eyed shadows
hopping like squirrels
through the greenless branches
of my immediate apprehension.
I remember when they died.

Stand amazed, now,
watching them haunt
reflections of their former lives.

The tourists hear one story
but let me tell you another:
like the one about WillieMae
who had 14 children, 9 they say
still living, just like she is
a blackwoman working split shifts
at what used to be the old
Desoto Hilton Hotel.
14 children, 9 still living
spanking, feeding, loving her brood
in-between preparing pastries
for people who'd rather not know.

But her story contains no irony
the husband died a death that was actual
and non-literary, her southern blackwoman's
life failed to reflect
the bohemian aesthetics of drag queens,
singers, and polka-dotted eccentrics
that made John Berendt's garden party
glow so lusciously with decadence.

I could tell the story
of that scar, on WillieMae's right leg
where police dogs
attacked like Klansmen
because she insisted that her children
laugh like anybody's children
in the sun-caressed green of Forsyth Park.

But that history has not been preserved
like the architectural jewels
that adorn a shameless hypocrisy.
Nor has it been dramatized
at festivals or parades
stirring up the ghosts on River Street.
Nor immortalized
by a Ray Ellis watercolor
or a statue in the center of a square.

We could even flip this coin
of WillieMae's tale
and recite the parable of how
she fed an entire neighborhood
with one fried chicken
and Jesus came back just to tell her
"WillieMae you did my recipe proud.
Hear what I say girl?
You did my recipe proud."

Shall we speak of that woman's biography
like a hidden chapter of this city's life
or shall we simply point
at a stupid little Hitch Village boy
feet covered with red dirt
and blackberry stains,
snot flowing like panic and river water,
some curious doctor's fingers
lost between his thighs
his dreams containing just enough genius
to save his mystified ass
from everything except
the slow knowledge of why
certain days stink putrid with agony.

Memories: vicious like a thicket
burning hot with cobras.
The wrong step
or an erroneous beat of the heart
and a man like me
could turn into a tower stinking with death.

31

WillieMae Sketched in Years of Blue

I.
Colorwise, your earth-lovely hands
are nothing like
the dispassionate blue gaze
of bare evening sky weeping
revelations at your feet.
But the ambitious immensity of it
is very much
as your hands once were
loving one infant after another:
7 boys and 7 girls,
wrapping the blanket
of your blackwoman's reality
around each of their minds
the way the air and heat and clouds
of this planet
circle oceans and continents
with their affections,
so have you cradled
our sorrows and glee.

II.
Some of us you saw blossom
then whither beneath
the merciless sun of oppression.
These are the facts minus sentiment:
3 of the boys, 2 of the girls,
your womb a victim
of america's fondness
for dead black babies,
3 boys dead, 2 girls dead,
your mother and father, 4 brothers dead
and both younger sisters all
citizens now of the grave
and yet through your body
entire generations have crossed over
to defy the illusion we call death.

III.
Your children stare at you now
and find themselves confused
by their split perceptions
of a woman whose dwindling form
mocks her expanding spirit.
4 pills just to say good morning.
75 units of insulin
to help you manage a smile
and we keep looking in your eyes
as if staring down a road
searching for images from your past:
a much younger mother
5-feet-11, jet-black hair
flaming like a river down your back
so much pride in your steps
that someone named you "Chief"
and proclaimed you ruler
over all things humane.

Your children find themselves confused
by their split perceptions of you.

But the one singing entered last
through the gates of your flesh
and the singer sees you
as you have always been:
an African womanchild
running naked through a village
with ghosts crackling in your hair;
a little wisegirl preacher
in the backwoods of Georgia,
chewing on lightning and spitting out prophecies;
a celestial amazon, so far from home
so far so far so far from home,
your soul looks back
and wanders past Jesus.

The singer is looking at your hands
and the sky flowing beneath them.
Your years are begging to be held
and it is time to make time for you.
Bathing my arms in the waters of this prayer
it is time to make time for you.

the brother, the keeper
(blue words for his soul)

you treasure your ignorance more than
i do mine. you worship its power
to absolve you --in the grandest tradition
of drunken priests-- from all responsibilities
while i hold no vision of its blessings,
only the chasm-like crack it creates
upon the continent of my soul's lonely yearning.
because you refuse to acknowledge your
creations, whether plant mineral or otherwise
your children learned to spell the word "feast"
at my table instead of yours. your lack of
respect for compassion's kingdom has caused
your mate to linger longer than she should
upon the bridge of my suspicious company. you like
your pigs' feet fried at three in the morning;
i prefer mine trotting happily raw in the forest.
surely it is fair to say you are heavier than
any elephant or building on this planet. an
abnormal mass evolved from abnormally chilling lust
for too much of everything: sex, liquor, hidden
smells of yourself. everything. supposedly my
flesh has been reinforced by spirit and made
strong enough to conduct all the heat you constantly
generate.   why does it never feel that way?
i think of us as elements within an impartial
equation, then suffer guilt for utilizing powers
that clearly maintain the miles of skin separating
us. our hearts. our minds. our funky false impulses
to love. nonetheless, there it is, neither
of us a total, a balance, a dividend or what pi
squared becomes. neither, sadly --or no?-- the problem
nor its solution. simply symbols like plus or
minus <but never greater than or less than, never
those> patiently awaiting the arrival of
something equivalent to peace in our lives.

Lost in My Father's Room

1.

In my father's room there are no doors leading to the shelter I
built separate from his 15 years ago and the two windows
that scar this very personal architecture look out on all man-
ner of wonders, there is a horsefly giving birth to an actual
horse and a weeping willow so heavy with tears that a salty
lake has formed around its trunk but do these have anything
to do --do they?-- with what happened when I stumbled and
stepped into a pair of my father's old bedroom slippers.   I fell
against the wall and found myself facing a wallpaper pattern
with hundreds of ears, human ears, black and white and yel-
low ears, elephant ears and bird ears, perfumed ears and
porcelain ears all of them spread across the wall as if the
designer thought they were wings or as if they were the true
tangible nature of sensitivity and I thought to myself: Ahh
well, this is really fine I tell myself, your willingness father to
listen now that you are dead and I am no longer in need of
your understanding.

2.

But I choose to reconsider when I scramble away from the
wall and end up sliding beneath your bed.   The entire bottom
of the mattress is shaped like a giant nose and I recognize it
as yours by the sand-colored birthmark on your left nostril.
It is shaped like North America on a map and I can recall
how a sneeze from you would appear to throw the entire con-
tinent into revolution.   Flat on the floor beneath the bed
where your giant nose flares and threatens, I am certain you
can smell within my veins the moonlit soul of the woman I
love, for we are precisely that close and yes I do become help-
less wondering whether you approve.   Do you approve?   Or
perhaps you sense the shape of the man whose life gloves
around mine like an exoskeleton placed sentimentally
between my heartbeat and the chainsaw cacophony of this
world's barbaric sophistication.   And what do you think of
that?   Of what you sense?

3.

I roll quickly from beneath the bed but that is how it goes for an entire day that lasts a full four decades, each time I move to leave the room I encounter a piece of you pretending to be a Freudian implant. There are your toes scattered like dead cockroaches all over the floor. Both of your eyes hanging from strings in a corner of the ceiling and your mouth taped to a ragged lampshade. I run inside a closet and your hands slap one side of my brain while your voice pisses acid on the other. I jump out reaching for a telephone and there is your penis, the unmerciful shocking reality of it, fully erect and dripping images of everything I've promised myself I shall never be.

4.

And it remains just as I said. There are no doors leading to the shelter I built separate from yours. What I discovered, of all things, was a staircase, leading to an attic, leading to a roof, where I did not bother searching clouds for the wings you never gave me. I took my seat on the edge, and out of nothing but spit, the dirt beneath my fingernails and carefully removed skin, I began to make my own. It could take another 15 years I knew or at least until the next morning. But once finished, they would be strong enough to snag a breeze going elsewhere, to lift me far above this room, should I start to stumble. Or fall. Or remember.

Church of Flesh and Smoke:
My Black Body Remembers

Once my body was the church
where Saturday nights
you crawled over the mahogany pews
of my legs and arms
then rocked in the pulpit
of my terrified cock
while I suffered your hymns
grunting spit against my chest
until hallelujah would have
no part of us. Damnation paid
for a most glorious ride
and hallelujah had no part of us.

Sunday mornings you did not
open the giant doors to
my sacred meanings
but copped one last feel
stuffing my genitals
apple-like down my throat
then lifted high your baby boy
to watch my story burn,
poured another jar of 'shine
watching my black story burn:

ashes swirl the sky
of our double remembrance
like exploded pieces of stained glass reality
and look.' LOOK AT THAT!
There's a painted memory
of you and I sitting naked
inside each other's blood,
and look, another image of me
and your sister behind the outhouse,
you and my brother beneath the back porch,
my daddy and your daddy
blowing reefer-rings in VietNam,
look at my mama's big black hand
bigger than the Confederate flag

wiping first your mouth then loving mine,
my mama's hand softer than vulva
spanking your white ass black
then beating mine blue.

Exploded pieces of stained glass reality
exploding pieces of stained glass reality
please explain this picture of you
burning churches with one hand
while diddling your dick with the other.

Fire is the water in which
history purifies itself.
Bigotry is a self-consuming fire
in which purity becomes obsolete.

blackman sitting on a rock

madness like a sugarcoated bruise
paints your face the same
color as frozen lava.

affection is a dead angel
adding up history's betrayals
in the center of your soul's ponderings.

your smile a poem
sung in languages
you have never understood.

I Can Hear Juba Moan

> "I find myself suddenly in a world in
> which things do evil; a world in
> which I am summoned into battle; a
> world in which it is always a ques-
> tion of annihilation or triumph."
> Frantz Fanon
> *(Black Skin, White Masks)*

Juba lay still on his belly, peeping over the edge of the fire
escape's platform at the three figures below him. They were
completely lost in each other's tangled limbs and he knew that
now would be the best time for him to climb back up to the
Hotel Haven's roof, but he was entranced and could not steal
his eyes away from the scene down in the alley.

He'd been on his way from the rooftop, where he'd watched
sea gulls flying homeward and stars popping into the early-
evening sky, when he stopped on the fire escape to watch a
bright ball of light. It sat over in the west, just above the hori-
zon where the sun had fallen and left traces of crimson in the
sky. The bright sphere outshined any star and Juba immedi-
ately recognized it as the planet Venus. He stared at the
sparkling planet for a moment, then remembered he'd been on
his way home, down to the hotel's basement apartment, where
he lived with Elijah. He wanted Elijah to see the book he'd just
read on "colonialism in twentieth century America" and maybe
get him to answer some of the questions that were tumbling
through his head.

The alley was dark, except for where a yellow patch of light
shone from the basement window. As he reached the metal
platform above the alley floor, Juba heard the scuffling of feet
and became still. An old man, short and bent, was digging in
a metal trash bin while three shadowy figures came down the
alley from the street. As they got closer, Juba saw they were
two men and a woman. One of the men hit the old man dig-
ging in the trash bin with a stick and sent him whimpering out

of the alley. The squeaky sound of the woman's voice scraped across the air and Juba quickly dropped to his knees on the platform.

"Why we had to come back here? Why y'all ain't just let me drop it in the trash can like always? Here, take it!" The voice was liltingly feminine and strained to display dignity.

Juba saw the small hand extend a wad of dollar bills. He chewed softly on his bottom lip as he watched one of the men finger the money but leave it in the woman's hand. They moved closer to the hotel's wall and he could see they were policemen.

"What's wrong, New Yawk honey? Thought you'd feel at home back here. Be just like old times befo you went away and I got married. Remember?" He was a stout, bullish man, his voice lazy and thick with intimidation. He ran a blunt finger from the extended money's tip to New York's wrist and traced the invisible line on up her forearm.

"Besides," he said, "too dangerous to handle money on the open street these days. Decent folks just ain't safe no more. Ain't dat right Charlie? ...I said ain't dat right Charlie?"

"Uh yeah, sho is Sam. Got so's a man gotta do his business in the dark."

Sam placed his finger on New York's right breast. She stuffed the money inside his shirt pocket, behind his badge, then moved to walk away, but both men blocked her path. She turned towards the alley end and cursed the brick wall that cut off her exit. When she turned around, Sam grabbed her right arm and Charlie grabbed her left.

Juba sat still, silent, watching.

"Don't do this to me Sam, pleeease," said New York. "I got customers waiting. You wanna mess up my business? Come on now. I know my rights you know..."

Sam gripped the strap on her right shoulder with his index finger and pulled it down her arm. The dress was low-cut, intended to show all but the tips of very healthy, very supple breasts. With one long stroke of his finger, Sam pulled the dress down and it fell around New York's ankles like a deflated balloon, leaving her naked of everything except the spiked heels on her feet.

"I'm gonna scream. I swear it."

"Why? Cause my name ain't Joseph Whitfield an I don't own no Jewelry store? What's the matter, you thought I didn't know about that little set up down at the Hilton?"

41

Charlie, tall, slim, and grinning, was on his knees with one hand trapped between New York's clenched legs.

"...I die tomorrow, hell gon take us together. Charlie don't.. don't do that...Sam, make him stop, make him...ooooooohh-hh..."

Her protests died away and gave birth to a chorus of groans and sighs tossed carelessly on the hot alley breeze. When they were done, Juba, still lying on his belly, watched the policemen pull up their pants and smooth out their shirts as New York lay sprawled on the ground, propped up on her elbows.

"Y'all ain't had to be so rough," she said, sounding tired and breathless, like she'd just washed a tub of clothes by hand.

"You southern boys still don't know how to treat a lady. In New York, I had a gentleman drop a pearl in my, uh... treasure box, every time he visit me. Don't suppose one'a you swine got a pearl."

She spread her legs wide and smiled as the men let out chuckles.

Juba began crawling backwards on the metal platform, groping for the ladder that would carry him back to the roof. He didn't want to take his eyes off the figures below him. He reached for the ladder but missed it and felt himself about to fall. Floundering, he grabbed the ladder's side and his elbow banged against the metal railing.

"Who's that?!" cried Sam in a whisper, spinning around and pulling his gun from the holster. He held it with both hands, pointed up, then stood back for a wider view.

"Hey, I see you nigger. Git your ass down here before I blow it away."

Juba stood up and leaned steadily against the ladder.

"What the hell!" shrieked New York, scrambling to get into her dress. "He been lookin! That nigger been lookin at me!"

"I said come down here boy, else I'm gon see how good you catch a bullet!"

Juba moved to the edge of the platform and held his hands up to show that he was not armed. He laid on his stomach, slid over the platform's edge and was about to drop to the ground when a large hand gripped his bare ankles and jerked him down. His arms and legs flowed smoothly out and he landed stealthily on his hands and feet.

"You see that Sam?" muttered Charlie. "He land just like a cat. Just like a cat."

42

As he began to stand, Charlie kicked Juba in the side and he rolled over towards the hotel wall, clutching his ribs and panting softly.

"Goddamned nosey nigger!" said Charlie, and he moved to kick Juba again, but Sam held him back with a hand on his shoulder.

"You been spying on us boy? What all you saw? What you doin up on that fire scape?"

Juba stood still in his silence, looking at Sam, whom he could see much more clearly now. A blond man with a thick mustache, and dark, hooded eyes. He's dangerous, Juba thought. Too dangerous. Something about the condescending smile on Sam's lips as he played with his mustache told Juba the man took himself very seriously, especially before people he considered his inferiors. It was not good that a seventeen-year-old black boy had caught him wallowing naked and shameless, like some drunk and naked Noah, snared by the laughing eyes of Ham.

"Damnit, he saw me!" screamed New York, now clothed and spitting anger. In a movement so swift that it blurred, she leaped past the two policemen and came down on Juba, beating him on his shoulders and head with the spiked heels of her shoes. He fell to the ground and curled into a ball.

"He saw me! Kill him, kill him!" screamed New York as Sam dragged her away by the hair.

"Can't y'all see... he laughing at us," she said, her voice becoming a limp, broken sob as she fell to her knees and freely cried.

Juba held his head up and stared into the barrels of the two guns pointed at him, then he looked into Sam's eyes. He slowly stood up, his back against the wall.

"I don't think he can talk," said Charlie. "That's that dumb nigger. Yeah, I seen him at Mama what's-her-name, giving all kinds'a funny signs to um, um--"

"Mama Bessie. I didn't know you eat there too. You sure this him?"

"Yeah. I remember cause he got all that curly hair, and see, he barefoot."

Sam noticed that not only was Juba barefoot, but all he wore besides his jeans were a denim vest and heavy flat gold chain around his neck.

"Can't talk, eh? Well I'm sure you know the position boy, so don't wait for an invitation to take it."

43

Juba lifted his hands to communicate with them in sign language, but when Charlie stepped towards him, holding his gun like a club, he quickly turned around and put his hands against the wall. The basement was a few yards to his left and he strained his eyes at the corners, hoping to see some signs of Elijah. Then his legs were kicked apart and he leaned harder against the wall, spread-eagled.

"You should'a stayed home tonight," said Sam. "Everybody know how horny niggers git after dark. Why you attack this here white lady? You couldn't be satisfied with tryin to rob the hotel. No, you got greedy like a prize hog and this just ain't your night for bein greedy."

Juba wanted to say something, but all that slipped from his throat was a slow animal-groan. He turned around a little and the butt of Charlie's gun smashed across the side of his face. He staggered slightly and hung his head down. Blood slid down his face as hands reached around his waist, unfastened his jeans and dragged them down past his knees.

"Had to make sure you ain't had no gun in there boy. What you lookin at New Yawk? Turn your damn head an act like somebody's molested mama. Turn your head I say! Ok Charlie, put the cuffs on 'im."

2.
"Who's that sweet young thang? Stick him in my cell!"

"Gotta smoke buddy? Say buddy, gotta smoke?"

"He's innocent! But of course we all know this. Jailing black men has become a sport in this country. Object of the game is to see how fast we become an extinct species, but I've got a news bulletin for you..."

The pleas and mumblings and half-jokes of prisoners fell around Juba like a steaming rain. He was in the Bison County Jail, walking down a corridor of cells with a guard who kept poking him in the back. The rank smell of urine burned his nostrils and made his eyes water. The walls seemed to stretch out for miles like an endless smoky desert, then suddenly shrink back and almost crush him in a box. He felt as though he would never wake from this whirlpool dizziness.

He was pushed forward into a cell. He stumbled, then slowed to a stop and ran back to the door of steel bars but the guard had already disappeared. The cell was small, filled with a grey dimness, with two bunk beds against the wall and a tiny barred square window. *He raped me. I was walking on the sidewalk, on my way to the drugstore when his hand grabbed me like I was some rag doll and pulled me in the alley.* Juba walked over to the window and sat down with his knees drawn up to his chest. He began to hum to himself. *We heard her screamin an caught him in the saddle, so to speak.* The light of the full moon poured through the window and showered him in a stream of silver-blue. *He's dangerous, been hearin things about him for some time now.*

No one had given Juba a chance to explain anything. The only sympathetic face he had seen was that of an old man, a janitor smiling sadly from behind his broom. As he sat humming beneath the window he thought he heard his father's voice but knew it was only an echo, risen from the canyons of a buried memory, reverberating softly within himself. He wondered if the jails that his father had spent so many nights in after "marching for his freedom" were anything like this one.

He recalled the two of them walking the hundred miles from Augusta to Stonestown, where Juba was to stay with an old friend named Elijah while David, his father, went north "to see a man about a flag." It took them a week to reach Stonestown because they traveled through the woods, camping near rivers or streams when they could. It was a holiday journey and every night David would teach Juba the names of different stars and constellations while they sat on rocks or lay in their sleeping bags. On their last night in the woods, Elijah came to the camp, and the next morning walked with them into Stonestown. Juba was awed by the man, seven feet tall, all of him thin lean and hard, with skin almost as dark as the tight cap of hair on his head. He wore a long leather strap around his neck. "It's a sling, in case the bears or other wild animals get to close." Juba looked at David to ask if there were really bears in the woods; he said nothing. The night before David left, Juba lay on a cot in the Hotel Haven's basement and listened while his father spoke with Elijah:

"...you'll think I'm bragging Elijah, but aside from being really bright, Juba's just special. In the same way his Mama was special."

"Some of the smartest people in the world never talk cause they got more sense than everybody else. I bet you ole Juba just fakin us out so he can--"

"Now you're joking, but there's something about him... Remember how Ruby used to make up songs and sing to herself? Couldn't nobody put the birds to shame like my Ruby. Right after Juba was born, she made the doctor bring him to her. He didn't want to cause we knew she was weak.. .and dying. She took that gold chain off her neck, put it on Juba and lay there singing with him in her arms until she died. That song she sang, it scared me, so full'a heaven and hell at the same time. Sometimes, I can hear Juba in his room at night, and he's moaning, or humming that song."

"So he inherited his Mama's musical talent. That's not unusual."

"It's not the talent that bugs me. It's the song. Who taught it to him Elijah? And don't tell me it's just coincidence or something fancy like subconscious memory. Nobody remember something they only hear once at the age of sixty minutes old. I think Ruby looks after him Elijah. I truly believe her spirit watches over him."

Elijah stared blankly at David, then smiled concedingly, and with that smile, gained permission to change the subject.

"Is King gonna be in Detroit?"

"Not when I get there, but he supposed to come after me and some others set up a few workshops and teach the folks how to handle themselves during the demonstrations. Detroit's been like a bottle of nitro these past few months, just waitin for somebody to shake it up so the whole thing can go BOOM. Gonna be rough, too rough..."

"I still don't understand why you took up with that crew David, trippin all over the country beggin for civil rights like a bunch'a monks beggin for bread crumbs. That ain't gon get us nothin but a lotta broken heads and early graves."

"Spare me Elijah. We been down this road a thousand times before and we always come to the same fork, so don't get started. I don't want to hear you bad mouthin Dr. King."

"No, I won't bad mouth your precious King. The man has stirred the people to action. A kind of passive surge forward maybe, but action it is. None of my criticism can take that away. I just wish he would make human rights the center of his program instead of civil rights so the rest of the world will start giving a damn about 'us po black folks' in America. I mean look at it David, by focusing on civil rights, he makes our struggle a strictly American issue, makes it look like a family squabble, but you and me know it run a lot deeper than that. And I don't know about this nonviolence thing either. Seem to me like Brother Malcolm struck gold when he said--"

And they talked that way until long after Juba had fallen asleep and their voices became like shadows hovering on the edges of his dreams. The next morning, he was awakened by David kissing his forehead and telling him to be a good man until he returned, which was sooner than anyone had expected. He came back one month later, both eyes closed and his body frozen, already prepared for burial. Detroit newspapers said he'd been accidentally shot while standing near a man who drew a gun on policemen raiding a blind pig "That's an illegal, but long-accepted after-hours joint, like the basement speakeasies in Philadelphia and New York," Elijah explained to Juba.

"Liars!" he yelled, standing with Juba in the churchyard where David had been buried. His voice was sharp and burned with bewilderment and pain. "Snakes don't bite as fast as those papers lie. Even if Brother Johnson hadn't written me, I would've known the truth. I would've known David wasn't in no blind pig. He couldn't even smell beer without throwing his guts up cause alcohol was his daddy's demon and it made David run like a rabbit... it made him run Juba." The giant frame kneeled down, closed his eyes and rubbed his forehead with a fist, as though trying to grind to dust the truth of his own words. "Why'd he have to stop to help that woman pick up money? What he want to try and calm down a white woman for while she screaming everything but murder? He from the South...supposed to know...they shoot niggers for shit like that..."

"I'm sorry Juba. Don't mean to make you cry." And at this, his voice lost some of its steel, it became light, became free. "You don't have to cry. You with Elijah now. I will teach you, like a man named Yoruba once taught your daddy and me. Did David tell you about Yoruba? Well, sooner or later, I'm sure he would have. I'll show you a trick Yoruba taught us, a thing old Africans used to do with their eyes. And I'll show you how a janitor like me fights his little wars with a typewriter. That surprises you, eh? Yeah, well I'm not quite the secret guerrilla your daddy made me out to be, though I have friends who...well, I have friends. We try to be cool and more brains than bullets or bombs, but sometimes the pressure comes down hard, then the heat goes way up into the hundreds, and even icebergs sweat when it gets that hot Juba."

47

3.

The dry rustling of sheets and the rusted squeaking of bed springs pulled Juba's attention away from the window. He had thought he was alone in his cell but was not surprised when he saw a man sitting on the top bunk.

"Stop makin that noise boy! This look like a goddamned funeral home to you?!"

The man lifted himself from the bunk and dropped loudly to the floor. As he walked closer, Juba stared, his eyes unblinking, unafraid, wide open like a fawn peering though forest dark.

"What's yo name? Whassa matter, can't you talk? Answer George when he talkin to you!" His voice was deep and boomed through the air with a ripple. Juba stood up. George was about an inch shorter than he, but built wider, like an ape, with a slight lean forward like one also. He was a red-skinned black man with his top front teeth missing, a scar across the bridge of his nose and reddish-brown hair.

"I asked you a question niggah! Can't you talk?!"

Juba shook his head, put his hand over his heart while shrugging his shoulders to apologize, and went back to the window. He looked at the stars again, to see if he could find the constellation Cassiopeia, a group of stars representing the beautiful queen of Ethiopia sitting on her thrown. Because it was July, she would be somewhere in the northern sky.

"Last man turn his back on me like that got it split open you barefoot punk! What's that round yo neck?"

Juba was in luck. As he stood near the window's side and looked out beyond the top corner, he could see the little dipper and its sparkling handle was pointing straight at Cassiopeia. Five of Cassiopeia's stars were in the shape of an "M" and he could tell the time by checking the position of the star at bottom left. It was almost midnight.

A big hand grabbed Juba's shoulder and spun him around.

"Look at George when he talkin to you! This gold round yo neck? Why they let you keep this chain? Ought'a get me enough cigarettes for two weeks, maybe some hash too. Give it to me."

Juba's eyes were like two dark moons, showing no light of comprehension or interest. He looked as though he'd gone to sleep and forgotten to close them.

"I said give it to me!"

George grabbed the chain and jerked it as hard as he

could, causing Juba's head to bang against his shoulders. He then pulled the chain towards him while gripping Juba's hair and pulling his head backwards as though he were a strongman trying to tear a telephone book in half, the pages of which were Juba's head and neck. The chain bit into Juba's skin as he tried to remove it from his windpipe. Juba struggled to swallow air back into his deflated and thirsting lungs. George pulled up then down, he tried to bite the chain off with his back teeth but merely broke a tooth and still the chain stayed on. Juba heard drums in the sweep of his half-consciousness, then the room was spinning and it went dark, light exploded and the room spun again. George finally released him and he fell to the floor sucking in air like a vacuum.

"Ain't gon kill you for no chain. Cost me more years than it worth. Besides," he said, his voice becoming soft, urgently tender, "that little chain look pretty on you. You can say it's a present from me. Don't get up. Stay right there. Stay on the floor and show George how grateful you is."

4.

New York ran her fingers through the hair on Joseph Whitfield's stomach as her hand lay on his chest. She kissed his breast and bit him on the nipple. He winced from the pain and dribbled a small groan of passion.

"You never told me why you were late," said Whitfield. His round belly shook as he spoke and ran his fingers through thinning brown and grey hair.

"I did tell you sugar, said I had business. Didn't know it was gon take as long as it did, but I made it up to you didn't I? Didn't your 'little diamond girl' make every second worth your wait?"

She moved her head up to his and kissed him hard on the mouth. He reached to hold her but she suddenly pulled away and jumped up from the bed. She stood smiling over him, teasing him, enjoying the helpless look of give-it-to-me on his face.

"I know you see other men, but the deal is you keep yourself for me on Fridays, and nobody but me. Nobody!" He yelled the last word and the sound of his raised voice bouncing off the wall startled him. He sat up and looked around as though someone else had shouted then he suddenly became timid. "Please, you don't realize how, how bad, I need to see you when I walk through that door... it's like a hunger...I-I feel like a puppy that's been chained up all week and need something good to chase. I'd trade my wife for you if I could. She could have my house and car an money if I could put you in a crystal cage with the other pretty little stones in my jewelry store. I wish for that."

New York opened her mouth to say something when the window shade rolled up and cut her off with its loud flapping. She walked naked over to the window. As she reached to pull the shade down, she saw a tall dark man standing beneath a street lamp, winding his right arm like a fastly spinning windmill. She put her hand to her mouth as the man's body suddenly heaved forward and a tiny spark of fire lit the air just before the stone struck her throat with the force of a rifle bullet. She grabbed her neck, stumbled backwards and fell onto the bed. Blood gushed into her mouth and spurted out onto Whitfield's legs and stomach.

"Oh my God!" he whispered. "Miss New York! Miss New York you're bleeding!"

He rolled from the bed and scrambled into his clothes while on the floor on his knees. The blood on his stomach seeped through his shirt. He grabbed his suit jacket from a chair and crawled until he got out the door. He ran so fast that he shot past his car and went blindly into the street, jumping into a taxi that almost ran over him.

5.

"Little pretty boy, be nice to George. Look at all that hair on yo head. Like some pretty little female."

Juba's back was against the wall. As easily as a child lifting a doll, George scooped him up in a one-armed bear hug and slid his free hand beneath the waistband of Juba's pants. He squeezed him tighter and tighter, all the while drooling and kissing at Juba's face, groping feverishly at his flesh. Their lips came hard together when George saw the first flickers of flame. He dropped Juba and jumped back. There it was again. Flame. Crackling, jumping, alive in Juba's eyes.

"What you, what you doin?"

George could smell the smoke, felt it drifting from a cloud in his hair. He looked down and saw the red tongues of flame licking at his legs, and the sudden rush of heat began to eat him like acid.

"Sweet Jesus, it's burning me. Help me somebody!"

Other prisoners began to yell.

"Shut the fuck up George!"

"Hey Georgie, you buggin the new kid? Save me some."

"I'm on fire! I'm on fiiiiiiirrre!"

Horrified at the flames climbing up his body, he grabbed a cup and began raking it across the bars of the cell door. The other prisoners did the same, thinking it was a joke, liking the fun of it. Tin cups clanking against steel bars. Music.

George ran back to the toilet to throw water on himself, but he was too late. His reflection no longer showed flesh at all, only a screaming mass of fire. All he saw of his former self were his eyes, wide and terrified, surrounded by red and yellow flames that had swallowed him whole. He screamed, a yell so loud and aching with such pain that all the other prisoners became immediately silent and three guards came running down the corridor. They opened the cell door without looking in first.

George lie on the floor on his back, mouth twisted down, eyes so wide they seemed to sit on top of their sockets. A guard knelt over him, touched his throat and wrist.

"Lordy! He cold and hard... like stone."

"You mean he--"

"Dead as a brick, an I don't see a scratch on him."

Soon, the prison doctor came and said that though he was not sure for the moment, he believed George had had a fatal heart attack. No one paid attention to Juba as he sat in the moonlight beneath the window. The guards put George's body in a green sack and took it from the cell.

When everyone had gone, Juba began to moan, a soft sound like a mother humming to her infant. The song was even, hypnotic, it swayed in the air like a seductive cobra, then it wasn't a moan at all, but an urgent wail like the cry of an old-black-man calling from the deacon's bench. It flew high then low as it flooded Juba's cell and spilled out into the corridor. Prisoners yelled.

"Shut up! Somebody shut him up! He tellin on me! Don't, don't let him... tell on me..."

"What's that song boy? Come on now, I'll sing it with you."

The sound of Juba's moaning attracted the guards on his floor and they came running back to his cell to see what the problem was, but when they tried to open the cell door, they found that it was stuck. Most of them decided he could wait until morning and returned to their stations. Others said they should break the door down and remove him because he made them feel uneasy and was obviously disturbing the other inmates, perhaps they should put him in solitary confinement that very night. A crowd of nervous murmuring and frightened laughter gathered among the prisoners, while still Juba sang, a slow, wordless, bleeding tune.

6.

Sam parked the patrol car behind the police station. He grumbled noisily as he stepped out.

"Ever hear anything so stupid in your life Charlie? The captain calling us in over a damn nigger. Live and be amazed Charlie! Live and be amazed!"

"Sarge said he was causin a disturbance. Guess he figure we know somethin he don't."

"He said the nigger was makin noise Charlie, singin or somethin. I tell you what this is Charlie. This a trick. I know the captain, see? He still sore cause'a that fifty bucks I won in the poker game last Saturday. He a sore-ass loser an he tryin to trap me in some phony misconduct charge or somethin just to get even."

"I can hear him," said Charlie.

"The chump shouldn'ta played," said Sam. "Should'a stayed home with the missus where his wallet was half-safe. Know what I think Charlie, I think--"

"Shut up Sam! Listen! Listen!"

Sam gritted his teeth. Who the hell did that dumb ox think he was telling to shut up? But he kept his mouth closed. Then they both heard it, a soft trail of sound snaking through the night air. Sam thought someone touched his face and he jumped. Smiling nervously, he slid his gun from its holster and backed up against the car.

"Come on Charlie. Let's go see the captain an stop actin like a couple'a pussies!"

Sam laughed dryly as he and Charlie walked swiftly towards the station house, their bodies bathed in the yellow glow of street lamps, guns pressed tightly against their hips. Fear had completely erased their reluctance to go inside.

"What's that?!" said Charlie, and as he turned around, a long shadow arched quickly forward. There was a squishy thud and Charlie fell backwards, clutching at his face.

"Git up, Charlie! What's wrong with you?!"

Charlie reached up blindly, grabbing Sam's leg, then his hand dropped and he became still. Sam moved his hand from his face and saw a stone the size of an egg stuck where Charlie's right eye used to be. Blood poured from the side of the wound. Charlie's head shook, the stone fell out, and the orb of his crushed eye flowed out with the blood behind it. Sam felt his stomach erupt with nausea and he vomited on Charlie's chest. Then he jumped up, holding his stomach and aiming his gun at the darkness. There! He could see him in the street, his right arm raised high, beginning a slow twirl.

"Who that?!" yelled Sam. "I can see you!"

He fired the gun four times.

"Damnit, I know who you is! He shouldn'ta been been there. It ain't my fault. Nobody told him to look!"

The tall figure held both arms above his head as though he were holding an ax and about to split the ground beneath him. He jerked suddenly forward and a short, piercing whistle cut the still air. The stone struck Sam's forehead and split the top off his skull. Policemen came running from the station house, called by the earlier sound of gunfire. A crowd gathered around Sam's body.

"Jesus!" somebody said. And a sea of mumbling began to quickly rise.

7.

A middle-aged man with white hair and grey-blue eyes peeped into Juba's cell. After tampering with the lock for several minutes, he stepped aside and asked the short black man beside him to try his keys on the lock. The door opened. Juba stopped moaning when they entered the cell, but he did not look up immediately. He had been watching the constellation Cassiopeia, the queen of Ethiopia, once again, and thinking that it must be beautiful to sit on a throne made of the stars.

"I'm Captain Michaels," said the white-haired man, going over to the window to stand near Juba, who slowly rose to his feet.

"This is Turee Washington," said Captain Michaels, indicating the man holding a broom beside him. "He tells me he knows your father and has explained that a terrible mistake was made in your arrest. I've learned over the years to trust Turee in matters like this. I hope you can somehow find it within yourself to forgive my men, or at least cleanse your heart of any self-afflicting bitterness. You must understand that these are delicate, explosive times we live in, times when we do not always act as we intend and mistakes come easily so

53

that men--"

Turee pulled the captain's sleeve, and with a raised eyebrow, reminded him why they were there.

"Oh, yes...well, Turee will show you the way out."

Turee was silent as he led Juba through the jail. He let him out by a side door and stood in the doorway as he pointed to a man sitting on a curb half a block away. Then he spoke.

"I've heard a lot about you and I suppose we'll be working together someday. Glad I got this chance to help you out. Tell Elijah that Turee said hello."

Elijah stood up when Juba came beside him, and Juba thought that seeing him rise was like watching a tree suddenly stand. His leather sling dangled gently about his neck.

"You look tired little brother, about the way I feel. I hope you've been studying tonight and not playing around too much. Trying to raise you right and here you are staying out til past midnight. What I'm supposed to do with you?"

He put his arm around Juba's shoulders as the night closed softly around them and they walked slowly down the street.

Considerations: The Funky Thing About It

IMAGINE JUSTICE: as a happy masturbator,
and the picture loses its fuzz, drops its buzz
breaks out into a clarity worth falling in love for.

TAKE A WORD: like sociopoliticohistoriography, and you
might as well shove an earthquake up your ass, might as well
be sad and white, black and blue, Tom and Dick and Jose
too.

THINK OF EQUALITY: as a room with all the lights out
and your brain too busy igniting sunsets
to judge a book by who or what it chooses to cover.

TELL YOURSELF: that democracy is a pizza with everything
on it and never you mind how funky flow the farts that fol-
low: gobble up all ye citizens, gobble up and fart proudly.

STEAL 60 SECONDS: to drown so deep in courage that you
float all the way up to love's lonely island then kiss the best
friend you'll ever have, yes kiss the best friend you'll ever
have.

IMAGINE JUSTICE: as a happy masturbator
TAKE A WORD: like sociopoliticohistoriography
THINK OF EQUALITY: as a room with all the lights out
TELL YOURSELF: democracy is a pizza with everything on it
STEAL 60 SECONDS: to drown so deep in courage that this
poem makes enough sense for you to forget you ever heard it.

We Sang This for Shekhem

I am the diamond black
like sweet-soft-night loving himself,
the countless stars of my presence
illuminating the spiral of history's journey,
I am the jewel formed
of ancient myth and holy need,
my mother's sweat-burned laughter
my father's bloody seed.
Love me, and Wisdom will
claim you solely for her own.
Hate me, and Justice
all your Beauty shall disown.
Enigmatic, sensuous, and loving of God,
I am the diamond black,
a hotly–troubled ebony Sphinx—
perched like a timeless vision
in the crown of these golden beginnings.

Self-Knowledge in the New Millennium

You are the man newly arriving
at history's worm-ravaged door,
the woman whose shadows are salves
upon the bleeding breasts of the earth,
the infant whose heartbeat
floods every harp in Paradise.
Muscled like the Rockies,
nurturing like the Ohio
you can split a boulder or caress
a lily with equal finesse, exactly
thank you, as you damn well please.

Not a song of yourself but one
of many selves do you sing—
unity embracing multiplicity giving
glorious birth to individuality:
a clown whose buffoonery heals,
a poet whose rhyme resurrects,
the scholar whose thoughts fire lasers,
the child whose smiles breed gods,
the hope whose pain raises joy,
the joy whose hope flowers pain,
the father whose power shines wisdom,
the mother whose grace vibrates power.

Not a wasteland do you claim but a valley
pregnant with stones bursting into
blossoms and flies exploding into light:
Do you howl? Yes we howl!
Soulscreams out of Africa,
mindscreams out of Europe,
heartscreams out of Mexico,
this tasty gumbo of mixed up beauty
as sweet as Sister Moon straddling
brother Sun, bitter as a cheated womb
shouting fire at the ocean.

Yours is a heart split/thrown-away/fortified
where demons' eyes spit hot secrets
at the long cool gazes of angels,
where a lake of blood kneels
before thirteen golden thrones:
to this music only do you dance your dance,
by its rhythm rearrange your soul.
You are the carpenter just getting here
stumbling through history's barely hanging door;
from time's rusted hinges come squeals
like things of hell trapped in heaven,
one touch and a knob of starless night
turns evolves into a dawn
necklaced with two brand new suns.

A man newly-arrived and arriving:
the whir of your spirit speeds up
propelling cells and dreams alike
onto the next open stage, placing bids
and souls on the table, moving like fate
towards the emancipation of love in your lifetime.

A Letter Came Today

By way of an African wind
a letter came today.
It was not scribbled over
Hallmark fantasies or
popcultural postcards;
it was engraved on sweat-dyed scrolls
manufactured by centuries
of anguish, struggle, determination.

Its theme and meaning were as clear as burning
niggers in New York on a bright sunny day.

We-the-people read it in Germany
and our shouts crumbled walls;
We-the-people read it in China
and signed it with dragon's blood;
We-the-people read it in Poland
and our tears dismantled a nation;
We-the-people read it in Savannah
and listen now how freedom's bells are singing.

By way of an African wind
a letter came today.

Splitting the Adam
(or, How Music Entered My Life)

I split the atom of my European Self
and found within a celebration of harmony.
Infinite tribes of living light
molding and loving each other
into a single bright star of truth.
Hands and voices shaping one another
into the slender glittery beams
of a beauty suddenly fulfilled.

I split the adam of my African Self
and discovered inside ten thousand choirs,
a lattice of rivers dancing and splashing
through the valley of time's wicked humor.
One soul after another flowered into ecstasy
deep in the center of a forgotten love.
In the fire and the music and the destinies
of creation, we bound our joy
with the solitary brilliance of our unified song.

I split the atom of my heterosexual Self
and out flowed celestial treasures
spilling emerald pearls of hidden wisdom.
Petals of knowledge dripping with happiness
and hungry for the taste of the moon
pulled my nation from a murderous sleep.
Two by two we rocked each other's tears until
compassion drew our eyes deep inside her eyes.

I split the atom of my gay Self, of my Christian
Self, of my Jewish and atheist and Muslim Self,
I burned the adam of my male Self and female alcoholic Self,
my poor and rich and black and white and old young gorgeous
fucked up hurt that's too bad: Self. I fused together
every particle that looked or smelled like truth,
and that is who I took to be my lover.
I split every adam in my bloodstink universe
and entered the kingdom where Mercy rules all pain.

Portrait Of My Heart That Is A Nation:
We Don't Got No Independence

1.

My heart is a nation born of much blood running wild, born
of nuclear opera singers screaming down the veils of nonreal-
ity, born of Jesus' eyes pressed flat against my astonishment,
my heart is a nation born of teeth gnashing like biblical
tragedies and hammers and nails reconstructing my barbaric
chest.

2.

My nation heart is fond of waging war against the toothpick
soldiers of its noodle-dicked ignorance. There is one battle-
field where emotions describe themselves as caucasoid.
Another where they are mongoloid and yet another where
they call themselves negroid. They wear each other ragged
like 501 Levis trying to oppress each others bodies and souls.
If the sun rises they cut each other's throats--then hide
behind trees. If the sun goes down, they fuck each other into
comas--then hide behind trees. The caucasoid/ mongoloid/
negroid people inside my heart are a nation of schizophrenics
for whom prozac promises no salvation.

3.

My bones are big big histories filled with big big lies. On
every other page I am there smiling, shoving my flag up
somebody's bum, staking unrighteous claim to his or her
shit. The way my heart beats is not always kind. Early this
morning I declared Love as a functional democracy now I am
stuck naked on a corner voting against my own simple-mind-
ed happiness, standing in line electing ignorance to rule over
wisdom.

4.

My astounding heart is a leader among nations but I don't
got no independence from all these slaves dying in the streets
of my soul. My bones are big big histories but I don't got no
independence from all these lies stinkin' up the streets of my
soul. My heart got a hundred dollar bill and the right to
remain silent but I don't got no independence from these rev-
elations bombing the streets of my soul.

Art, Love, Hunger

The shape of something uncaring and
perversely cold stands up inside a man
and he finds himself completely deceived.
Believing this world's anguish is something
different from the love he keeps holding back.

There is a story about a wealthy man who
gathered beggars from throughout the city
and took them all home. Thinking he would
feed them, they smiled and shined
like newly opened daisies praising the sun.
But the wealthy man did not feed them.
He grouped them closely together then
recorded the sound of their stomachs' loud rumbling.
He needed this sound he said to add a dramatic touch
to a waltz, a masterpiece, he was composing
for a special ceremony. Afterwards, he paid
each of the grumbling stomachs ten cents each
then took them back to where their sadness
and hunger lived. Later that night,
the wealthy man was dreaming about angels
when he felt someone cut off both his feet.
He woke up screaming just as a huge woman with a
huge knife grabbed his hands and chopped those too.
The woman cried and apologized but said she needed
his limbs to add realism to a special sculpture she was creat-
ing for a special event. She gave him a silver dollar for each
hand and foot then squeezed her bulk back out the window.

The shape of something uncaring and
perversely cold stands up inside a man
and he finds himself completely deceived.
This world's anguish is no different
from the love we insist on holding back.

Decision and Distance:
Playing With Evil

The muscles in my thighs flexed tight, relaxed,
as the bicycle rolled to a stop
at the top of a hill overlooking the city.
With the slow movements of a seducer
the evening sky removed its bright blue cape
and slipped into a negligee of lavender and ash.

Looking to the east, I saw a carnival
with ferris wheels and roller coasters glowing
inside the palm of this dreamy dreaming dusk.
And I was thinking I would love to be there.
I was breathing the sensuousness of the idea
that destiny or kindness might approach me
disguised as a buffoon and make me laugh
until I pissed flowers over everything in sight.

Then I turned west and there were six people
playing basketball in the sand and surf of a beach.
They played the game, but instead of throwing
a ball through the net, they were tossing
blue and black rattlesnakes six feet long.
And I had to admit the truth of their actions:
that we do indeed like to play with evil.
Even when it is dead and exhausted
we place our open mouth against evil's innocent fangs
and force it back to life.

I looked beyond the hills where the carnival shined,
then again to the beach where people played with evil
and it occurred to me that choices were waiting to be made.
Suddenly I was starving for the laughter of a friend.
The night hammered my brow like a judge without compassion.
And it occurred to me that choices had to be made.

A Mutant Quail With Kaleidoscopic Feathers
(Cliff Notes on loving a schizophrenic demon)

How many madmen sit inside your mouth
jacking off trauma, pretending it is genius
and what the hell are they so mad about anyway?
Whose ignorant intentions twisted your heart
into a feast fit for vampires?

Tell me about the madman that hangs your mother
upside down naked as a dog's dick in public
then whips her ebony spirit more brutally
than any slave master ever did your ancestors.

Or talk about the Tennessee Williams imitator
who wears his scars like pants made out of gonnorhea
dripping orange pus, and using your vulnerability
to manipulate those who give you their trust.

More interesting still is that one madman
who adopts the dead maggots in your mind
raises them into fully diseased falsehood then
sends them zooming off your tongue like little
u.f.o.s out to abduct everybody else's joy and comfort.

What is it about love that churns you into a masochist?
What is it about peace that explodes chaos straight up your
    nose?
At first glance you are a mutant quail with
Kaleidoscopic feathers more brilliant than a peacock's vanity.

At second you are all the worst moments in your own
biography, dozens and dozens of identical idiots all competing
to flood your mouth with the glamorized shit of their hyper
    realism,
one hundred loud-mouthed nonseeing madmen all claiming
    to be you.

I Am A Scar Talking Maximum Shit to Your Face

Imagine me as this riddle: what is five million-plus
square miles, crusted over with the dead skin of too much hate,
swollen unto monstrosity by the stink of a pus
that will not drain? What should we call this mixture
of life for the dying and death for the living?
Imagine me as this riddle then understand me as this
answer: I am a scar talking maximum shit to your face.

The weight of my country's heel snapping the neck
of my spine gave birth to my endless bleeding:
my father is a 3-foot canal whipped with precision
into the back of a black man. My father swears
he was born starving for the taste of my screams.

The sound of my nation's teeth grinding my heart
into a finely powdered cocaine gave birth to me:
my mother is a scalpel that slipped 9 inches
from yoni to navel. She wrote a poem comparing
my tears to moonshine said they made her skunk-ass drunk.

I am a scar talking maximum shit straight up your nose
blasting like a rocket out the back of your skull.

Call me the tissue of the evidence of things
well hidden, the pulse and echo of unvoiced opprobrium.
I am the wound that feeds on cyanide thought:
-- "I wonder if that nigger's been fucking my wife"
-- "I bet that cracker is ripping me off"
-- "Somebody ought'a rape that bitch and teach her a lesson"

I am a scar breeding lesions and cancers and dropped-off parts.
My eyes are ecumenical and multi-racial, multi-sexual, and
multi-disenfranchised. I am a scar talking maximum shit to
your face.

Imagine me as a riddle in search of rhymes to harmonize
my reasons. If I am agony that drinks champagne and strips
naked to cover another with my dubious intentions am I nev-
ertheless a civilized creature? My father is a 3-foot canal
and my mother a nine-inch cut from yoni to naval.
I am a scar dripping eagerness-to-love and forgive-me
and help and dripping and dripping and dripping...

Thus Spoke The Madman: How Louie Raged Waking Up Last Week

> "Never will the world be conscious of how much it owes to neurotics, nor above all of what they have suffered in order to bestow their gifts on it."
>
> Marcel Proust
> *(The Guermantes Way)*

What chu mean bus fare cost a dollar now? Since when it stopped bein thirtyfive cents cause that's all I got anyway. What?! Get off the bus?! Why the hell you wanna say somethin that stupid boy? You better drive this damn bus so we can all get to wherever we goin! And I bet chu stupid enough to think you got a clue, ain't it? You probably lost ninetyeight percent of your mind watchin filthy movies and jackin off last night then had the nerve to get up this mornin thinkin you knew where you was goin, believin with a bona fide belief that your intelligence was actually that exceptional.

Say what? Go ahead and call the cops if you wanna. All my friends and family already in jail and possibly my heart is grievin to see them. Possibly it sho nuff is, but now look at all these passengers waitin for you to drive this damn bus. Hey y'all, he say he ain't goin nowhere til I get sixtyfive more cents --SO!--if y'all want this thang to move... Why thank you ma'am, thank you so much sugar. And Lord look at this white man givin me fifty whole cents! Bless your heart boy! Bless your wretched little treacherous heart!

66

Lady why is you starin at me? I resent your eyes violatin my privacy in public. What?! I know I stink heffa! If you was sleepin up under a bridge for the past ten years your Last-Dollar-dress-wearin-flea-market-shoe-shoppin-high-damn-yellow ass would be stinkin too! Who knows how many times that tide came in and how much shit it dragged in with it? Who knows the uncountable corners of the earth or hell from which said mysterious shit came? Instead'a you freakin out about me smellin so funky, you ought'a be screamin over what a miracle it is that I'm standin here fuckin with your pitiful dumb ass.

But yeah, yes, it has come to my attention that the world ain't what it was when I knew it in the years gone bye and bye, but it just so happen that you talkin to a man who still is a man so I suggest you respect that fact and adjust your assitude accordingly.

Lo and behold --Bless the Lord-- they tell me these is the 1990s and my black ass is still breathin: I'm here on earth witnessin wonders to be lived and mysteries that astound. Just like right now I'm standin here lookin' at you black boy and you white girl, sittin there all cozy together with the metal rings in your nose, in your lips, in your ears and eyebrows. Y'all sittin there smilin at me but shouldn't you be on somebody's operatin table tryin to get those things off your face? No?! You don't think so? Well ain't that somethin? That's more than I know to say anything about. Hmph!

They tell me these is the nineteen nineties and here I done woke up and I'm talkin bout it y'all. I was walkin down the street this mornin and I saw this little boy on his knees bendin over some grass that was growin out the sidewalk. Well the little boy was just'a cussin at the grass and I mean he came up with some combinations that was downright addmyrable. But I had to ask him: "Little boy why you cussin at that grass so bad?" And you know what that little boy told me? -- He was cussin at the grass cause it was green. And he wanted it to be blue. I was so amazed that I almost did a number two right there in my drawers standin on the sidewalk lookin at that little boy cussin up a storm beneath a bright summer sun that only this mornin rose up like a bird out'a God's great remembrance when wasn't nobody lookin and you damn sure better believe my black ass was amazed. Lordy lordy, I'm tellin y'all!

Then I kept on walkin -- y'all understand this was before I got on the bus now, right, this was before the driver --bless his

67

slick ass, don't hit that car boy-- before he told me I needed a dollar when all I had was thirtyfive cents and that woman who done got off gave me a quarter and this man who still here praying for me to shut up gave me fifty whole cents and now he regret it cause I'm loose loaded and alive. I mean that shit just the way y'all heard it: loose, loaded and alive! That's...um, is nurse Pemblebrook on this bus? She usually bring my pills round about this time. She a big fat ugly bitch but she kind and she patient like somethin glorious out'a the Bible. Anybody seen her?

...Um, what was I talkin about before the recollection of your presence interrupted me? Yeah, that's right, I was walkin down the sidewalk and the wind of all this world's magnanimous incredulity blew a piece'a newspaper right against my face. It had a story in it about a man who raped a woman and beat her up real bad. Beat her up real bad y'all. He left her for dead but somethin more generous than him spoke up and made her to live. He didn't know for whom that bell was tollin as he walked away without lookin back. The newspaper say he went home, drank two or three beers and went to bed, then another man broke inside his apartment and robbed him and raped him too. Glory Jesus! Well don't y'all know old people used to say what go around come around but I think somethin done got out'a hand here! Why these people stickin their things inside'a other people without askin or nothin? That man forced his personal self inside that woman's sacred nature and I can't call that fuckin cause there wasn't no grace in their untimely togetherness. He ruled her body and crushed her mind until they threw up pure grief and then somebody else ruled his body and crushed his mind until he... did what? Until he did what? We come to an important aspect here:

Did he bleed and cry about diseases or pregnancy the way the newspaper say that woman did? Or did he reach an understandin about hisself the way we do sometimes when playing with mirrors, cause that's what the other man was like for him. Right? Like some kind'a dirty broken up mirror reflectin back all the dirty and broken up things he is on the inside and maybe on the outside too? But what I wanna know mostly is why somebody wanna stick a certain piece of hisself inside a certain piece of another human being if the other human being don't ask them to put it there and why does that communicate to his brain the word we call pleasure when his sperm had to feel and smell like cold mud from hell inside that woman, and that other man's sperm, that third real freaky corner on this shaky triangle, that other man's sperm had to feel and smell that way too, didn't it? Raging up inside that first man's ass? Damn, gonna rape some hard-legged bastard without prior knowledge to the particulars of his anus.

But chu know what I heard somebody say? I heard somebody say they saw the first man, the one who did the rapin and then got raped, down at the police station. And they was talkin bout how peculiar the expression on his face was. Why was they surprised? Seem to me like anybody who go to bed all by their saintly self then suddenly wake up with somebody else's nuts sneakin up their butt is bound to walk around for a while lookin mighty damn peculiar. Shit.

So here we had these two men and they was eatin some fierce wickedness cooked up on a woman's belly. From what I understand they didn't care nothin bout the reality of God bein inside every single one of them. God as woman inside the woman. God as man inside both those men. Nobody was touchin the other bodies with any kind'a divine music in their fingers. Just grindin out their self-concerned ultra nasty arrogance. What did they think God was thinkin, standin somewhere beside the independence of their human will. And did any of y'all passengers call your president and tell him to get his ass down here and cut this horrendous mess out?! Did y'all call the National Guard or the Marines? That's what happened when niggers tried to go to college some years back so seems like this would'a been a lot more scary.

Lady is you starin at me or listenin to what I'm sayin? What chu see anyway when you think you lookin at me? I been this big and this black all my displaced life and I know for a fact that my dick is not a creature from your nightmare mythologies, it is a friend to my grief and the carrier of my potential for an undiluted divinity. Is you still starin at me? What? Am I Emma Lee's baby boy? How the hell would I know who gave birth to me? If you ask me somethin that stupid again I'm gonna unzip my pants and rain all over your parade. Crazy people like you give insane motherfuckas like me a terrible name! You shouldn't be out in public by yo'self anyway. I think about what your brain is like behind that face and I get questionable just lookin at you.

Lord Lord Lord, this here is the nineteen nineties and I'm standin here talkin bout it, but one thing I know for sure, just as sure as I'm standin here smellin like a river full of chitlins,

I am a man, and something other than a man, something which moves and dreams in and out of different dimensions where sometimes planets such as black and white dance to the same drums, where jigsaw pieces like male and female solve the same puzzle when you touch them the right way.

But here we is in the nineteen nineties and... where's nurse Pemblebrook... anybody seen my old friend nurse Pem-- Hey bus driver! This my stop! Damnit did you hear me boy, I said whoa! Stop this bus immediately! Yes, thank you kindly sir. You understand that I would kiss you goodbye but who knows where all your mouth has traveled in its dubious lifetime. And then too there is the possibility of your falling in love and turnin into a nuisance. All y'all have a good day now, and don't be pissin me off the next time we share this journey together. We ain't got time for that.

The Light, That Never Dies

And now we step
to the rhythm of miracles.

The time of light is upon me
like dusk
pillowing its weary gray head
upon the pearl-grey shoulders of mountains.

Having known me too intimately
Grief turns away now
like a false lover burned
too severely.
The naked sentry
of a single true integrity
salutes the bold unfurling
of dignity's simple flag.

Fear crawls into the shadows
of the damned and wretched.
Peace blossoms like moonlight.
In the depths of a night
steaming and fetid with blood
a man stands perfectly straight,
    his eyes dancing among the saints,
    his heart singing for the angels.

Miguel Upon the Sand Dunes of Ecstasy and Hell
(Passion for the Shaman in 1994:
That Love Should Have Its Way)

Breathes burning sugar and frozen memory,
pumps holiness through each of his cells
while the sun squeezes his behind
and crumbles his spine
flips, flops, and rolls him back and forth
like a baker gone insane
slapping bread into crucified dreams of art.

His desert sky shines with goddesses
cooing clouds inside your ears
the air freezes with angels demanding
you stand up and glow like one true god.
Snakes in white tuxedos crawl rattling down your throat
and you shit poison for more days in hell
than you ever want to count again.
A dead butterfly makes love to your eyes
and you shiver semen wide across the wind's wide naked
tongue.

You are golden and rose like a beautiful ballet.
You are cold, demonic and hungry.
A storm gray and furious and white
is what your soul looks like
zooming in and out of your pitiful heart.
Look at her praying for you Miguel
and bleeding for you, loving God for you and
swallowing the whole history of His pain for you.

Miguel upon the sand dunes of ecstasy and hell
imagines he is Walt Whitman
cut straight in half by the beauty of soldiers,
dreams he is Malcolm X and Gandhi bleeding justice
inside the syphilitic mouth of a nation.
Believes he is ancient and Yoruban and female
splitting his body giving re-birth to his father,
provides comfort to ghosts fresh from their bones,
sets free the niggers in Alice Walker's nightmare
and sings her demons into well-earned death.

Miguel burns godly and shamanistic, his chest
studded with rubies, mouth foaming diamonds,
three black owls pour feathers on his head
and he yells into the night:
"I insist unrelentingly upon ecstasy
and I demand that Love should have its way
with all my Lord's creation."
Miguel walks hard-on bowlegged through the desert
shouting new light into this new sky
screaming loud Ezekiel's name.

Prophets kiss his tears, laugh hallelujah,
     get him stoned on wine.
Saints wash his blood, they all sing amen,
     tell Miguel to be quiet for a while.

A Spring Day in Konya

It is a spring day in Konya.
Sunlight sings like a bird
perched inside the glow of bronze minarets.
And yours are the eyes
skipping gleefully through my fear.
Your silence a mysterious tenderness
painting fields of poppies red like Mars.
As the goldsmith hammers his ore
angels take each other lightly
and float beside children going up
and down these stairways of heaven.

It is a spring day in Konya.
Your thoughts twirl like spiders
looming back and forth pulling the threads
and hairs of my existence
between the silk and velvet of a
dozen worlds and I can almost see
the final meaning of who I am --
There is an old man with hands made
of pure salvation and through their light
I can sense with intoxicating clarity
every single answer to my life.

It is a spring day in Konya.
Blue butterflies join the sugar merchants
singing with a sweetness greater than their goods.
Our king has drank too much mystical wine
and his mind staggers naked across the hilarious sky.
For as long as you are content
to embrace my heart inside this vision --
It shall remain a spring day in Konya
and everything that you touch,
shall be everyting I yearn to be.

From The Book of Aberjhani Dreaming:
Dancing With Rumi 4/18/95

The strongest dream I've ever had on the joys and principles of Sufi teachings in my life.

It showed myself and a Rumi-like figure dancing in an elegant whirling fashion, sometimes embracing each other as we danced, more often standing slightly apart. We were surrounded by school children and their teachers, who followed us as we danced. We sometimes moved on the ground then sometimes literally danced on and through the air, whirling full of gentle grace and beauty.

We went near the sea and I noted the significance of it as a symbol for free-flowing consciousness and the expansive cosmos.

From there we went to a housing project-like building with a staircase leading to the second floor. We moved up the steps with the children still crowding around us. We each stepped off to one side, standing on the air and preparing to descend as a demonstration of divine power.

We said to each other that it was "time for the sun and moon to change places."

It seems that I was the sun and he the moon, but as I meditate upon this, it feels more the opposite: that he was the sun which I was becoming and I was the moon that he was absorbing. And I sense too, that this change was to occur naturally.

Time to Be the Sun

Wake up pretty baby.
It's time to be the sun.

Time for us to drop
back down to earth
like old lovers
falling into new appreciation
for the soft mouth
of an attraction
that is no longer beautiful.

Open your eyes,
oh precious light.
It's time to cry
the glorious syllables
of our past,
time to thrash and moan like dragons
breathing hot
the secret songs of our future.

We are going to the valley
where roses blush naked and wise,
we are going to the mountain
where night rolls fiercely
with an uninhibited dawn.

Wake up pretty baby,
shine bright my summer joy,

Time to be the sun
    and send forth flesh
        to heal the bones of time.

Time to be the woman
    hauling up gold
        from a heart you thought destroyed.

Time to be the man
    you thought long dead
        buried in waters of tortured mind.

Time to be your own faith
    and give miracles to heaven.

Time to be your own truth
    and pull your ass up out of hell.

Time to be the sun
    and watch your soul rise pretty baby shine,
        rise pretty baby shine,
            rise pretty baby shine.

Washington Park #162

I once watched Time grow fat
then explode in my
face as if too much pain
or too much love had
gathered too fast into a single small space.

The Universe said, "Let me show
your soul something beautiful."

And I then recalled two things:
the Disciple who loved his Teacher,
and the main reason I was born.
I watched Time disappear and tasted
upon my fingers the colors
of a vision still hot with truth.

Past Present and Future Are One
(after a painting by Luther E. Vann)

1.

Memory, awareness and expectation: each of these a separate
highly fragrant blossom, their shapes different, their textures
different, the color of one black, another purple, and the third
silver. Yet all three growing on one giant vine of conscious-
ness in this garden of existence.

2.

The truth is there was not one but several wombs and several
seeds that gave birth to this entity that I presently am. History
is an hermaphrodite with many distinguished lovers. We are
neither mysteries nor strangers but the living breath of revela-
tion made flesh by the unrestrained desires of a free and uni-
versal love. Universal me. Universal you.

3.

"I remember," said a friend of my father's once, "when you
wasn't nothin but a gleam in your daddy's eye." And I had to
think about that. I had to wonder if my father had tried at
all to measure the possible power of that gleam before it
spilled from the story of his lust into the epic of my pain.
Yesterday's pleasure principle now over six feet tall and hun-
gry for more than a gleam can ever provide. Time is a wizard
that can pull either agony or ecstasy out of its magical hat,
depending solely on the hand behind the heart within the
eyes that gleam. Then fade.

4.

Time (again, Time) like the soul, wears many faces, many
bodies and climates and attitudes. The past is one face, the
present a second and the future yet another. Each of these
different yet stemming from a single root of divine conscious-
ness. I have observed souls teasingly dress themselves in
European skins with African sensibilities, or in feminine
forms with the masculine essence. The mind draws a
crooked line and convinces itself that this is reality. Prophets
speak of veils that cheat us out of the truth. In a rich moon-
lit garden, flowers open beneath the eyes of entire nations
terrified to acknowledge the simplicity of the beauty of peace.

Sunrise

I saw a sunrise bow in greeting before my brother.
The waning moon of his gaze focused
beyond the weeping and wailing of stars
falling like civilizations through my heart.
And the myriad insulting meanings of life
played upon his face like the spirits
of things I have never understood.

Out of the early morning light came
three slender beams of gold, and ruby and white
stepping through the window beside his bed
and taking upon themselves the forms
of something not quite human, not quite godly.
They exuded that brilliance barely suggested
in the paintings of this world's masters
and by their light I stared at the
hieroglyphic lesions upon my brother's face.

Within their empathetic glow shined the
side of my brother's life I'd never allowed myself to see.
I saw in their arms ready to attend his trembling
the hands of lovers and strangers he had known
and I felt in their compassion his constant
struggle to differentiate between the two.

On how many mornings did you compromise
your flesh, in the absence of another's
true affection? When? And how? And why
did your need for love become so expensive
that nothing less than your life
could pay its cold exorbitant price?

These creatures made of starbreath
and visions must have seen you
in those moments that stood like walls
of alien genetics between your life and mine.
They knew what you were like, vibrating
your entire universe against the skin and tears
of another, slowly crushing your skull

between planets of intolerance and desire.
And yet they do not hesitate lifting
your sleeping soul into their embrace
the way I always did before speaking
your name, or the way I do now --watching--
the inexplicable terror of my grief
staining your passionless eyes.

I saw a sunrise take my brother into its arms
and spread his colors across the sky, burning like butterflies
from one end of the wailing horizon to the other.

Through the Heat of Human Skin

Dust of a river fallen into disgrace,
and your eyes accusing my heart of murder.
On a road bending east towards memory and
misfortune, I am pursued by days with chains
on their feet, and I am offended
by the brutal tenderness of my spirit
pulling tears from the center of my brow.

I am a man with an agony of histories
seeking to alchemize air into stone
in order that I may shape it into
a possible future or a possible death.
What does it mean when my arms
stretch suddenly towards the sky
and I stand like a cross
begging forgiveness from the evening sun?
This riverbed echoes like a canyon
puking words from somebody else's century.

Ashes of a forest disowned by love.
And my lips caked with the blood
of this need for affection. I am a spirit
wrapped inside an ecstasy of possibilities,
wandering through a world addicted
to its hunger for clever cruelties.

I harbor the same suspicion towards
the man in a blue wall street suit,
hiding my scent inside his body,
as I do towards the robin-haired woman
using my flesh as excuse for her confusion.
The problem is: I find it easier to talk
with God through the heat of human skin
than to lie on Him for any reason at all.
I know exactly what it means when I hear
my back crunching like an embryo
between my brother's perfect teeth.

This forest smells like an oven
burning the bones of horrors too often indulged.

Dogbites and Bitches' Delight:
The Ft. Lauderdale Prophecy

My feet black and cool upon steps like the marble-white
shoulders of icebergs were much steadier than I'd thought.
The color white convinced me I was living some future
moment blessed with peace. And your body reposed in my arms
never stirred once, as step by sparkling step I moved
through hell's lovely evil, watching the hounds
of my demise gather around me like storm clouds
gobbling every shred of blue tranquility in sight.

Which of them jumped first I don't know.
Nor can I say how you remained alive in my arms.
I counted more than eight of them: dogs and bitches
of the strangest breeds: double-headed greyhounds
the size of horses. Alsatians striped like tigers
with tusks growing out of their eyes. Rottweilers
with the horns of bulls and the greed of piranhas.

One flashed in front of me and ripped the cloth
of my shirt. Another blurred near my waist
and drew blood from my genitals. A third
almost clawed your breasts and in your sleep
you turned to slap me 3 times.
I could have dropped you then and there.
Could have damned my failure at some later hour.

But to my left a woman shrouded in black gave her
mind and soul to bear witness beside my mind and soul.
The air around us crackled prophecies that one day
my spirit would heal my flesh and flesh glorify my spirit.
"Do not look at them. Maintain your gaze where I am.
As lashed and bitten as you are,
you cannot help stumbling, but you shall not fall."

Every step I took was a year vanished from my life.
And a paradise that breathed anew. For each move I made
the woman in black moved beside me, her silence like a
shield made of thunder. What I recall now is a memory of
children I once taught to bathe and read, and siblings
    whose love fed my heart.

As yet I can see rabid nightmares feasting on my ankles and
   hands.
The very last thing was a brilliance like the sudden creation
   of time.
The light of it stitching my parts back together
while easing your bewildered trembling out of my arms.
The canines yelping and humping in a far-off mirage.

To resist fear: has been difficult.
   And now the dogs chew each other's bones.
To believe in love: has proven dangerous.
   And now the bitches sniff their brains boiling down in
hell.

Crossing The Bridge of Bones

Just beyond our boiling hunger the sun
gleefully pushed a smouldering nose
between the ash-blue breasts of the horizon.
And night whipped us like mules toward
sorrow. With each step across the bridge
of bones our songs wept louder and light spilled
helplessly from the body of the angel curled up
like a leaf made of dreams in your hand.
Mirrors made of stone and old water
stared quietly down the tunnels of our past.
Skeleton fingers rose up from mud
to grab at flies and long lost poetry,
bones clicking and breaking like petrified lust.

"Is this your dream or mine?" someone asked.

The moon turned inside your eyes and opened his eyes,
cleared a throat made of pearl and said it was his.
Reflected at our feet were scenes of you in a white
nightgown, mopping up the blood of what had died.
Together our eyes hurried elsewhere and reached
the rotted carcass of an elephant. Stepping through
the bones of the beast a smell like honeysuckle
and shit inside a dead man's pants rose and shoved us
forward, blasting our steps with insane love and fury.
The angel nearly dropped from your hands as we stumbled
across the end of the bridge and fell before the gates
of a city neither of us had ever seen before.

Just above our terror, the stars painted this story
in perfect silver calligraphy. And our souls, too
often abused by ignorance, covered our eyes with mercy.

Shadows and Prayers and Light

> "But if only you could pause and remember as the shadows come closer that they cannot obscure the real light which is the light of the spirit... It is a hard lesson to learn."
> --Silver Birch
> *(The Philosophy of Silver Birch)*

The shadows' blatant disrespect for light nauseated Spencer Holliman to a point of speechlessness. But stronger than his outraged sense of logic was the fear that had grappled about the veins leading to his heart and that threatened, like iron hooks on a giant brick wall, to tear everything down.

He had spotted the first shadow when it was no larger than a mouse, crouched along the south wall facing his king-sized bed. Immediately he had switched on the three floodlights installed above the bed. Though the shadow had disappeared for several seconds, it had, to his dread, suddenly returned with several friends as large as cats, rapidly growing until they were as huge as bears, elephants, stepping away from the wall and reaching for him.

"JESUP! JESUP! They're back! They're back Jesup, don't let them take me pleeease!"

One freezing tentacle of black lightning nearly lashed his face when he threw his lunch tray at it. At the turn of the crystal knob on the bedroom door, the shadows zipped back behind the planes of light and corners of the walls from which they'd come. As he stepped into the room, Jesup's eyes fell first on the crescent roll at his feet, then skipped to an engraved silver fork, a shattered tea cup, saucer, soup spilled on satin sheets and on up to the slight trembling form of his employer. Shielding his eyes against the hot glare of the flood lights, Jesup looked about the room before calling out, "Mr. Holliman sir, I'm here."

Spencer slowly lifted his face from the crater he'd carved into the pillow. He looked from Jesup's face, quickly beading with perspiration, to the walls and ceiling. Seeing only the expanses of white throughout the room --he'd had all furniture save the bed and two night tables removed-- he sank back against the pillows, sighing heavily.

"Thank God!"

He feebly held forth one wrinkled arm sheathed in silk. Jesup walked quickly to the bed, retrieved a stethoscope and blood pressure gauge from the night stand, took the appropriate readings and reported them to Spencer.

"Very well, good, thank you. Thank you. Did you see them this time Jesup?"

"Just barely sir. As I opened the door, a pack of them seemed to dive behind it, then somehow disappear."

Spencer nodded eagerly at this corroboration of his ordeal, then stopped, uncertain as always during those rare times that Jesup agreed with him. Was that a smirk threatening to crack the straight humorless line of Jesup's mouth?

"But they're gone now sir. And I do have to admit my surprise at their presence in the middle of the day when the sun is at its brightest."

He switched off the floodlights and the brilliance in the room did, indeed, dwindle only a little. The sarcasm in his voice, italicized by the brutal click of the light switch, was this time unmistakable. Spencer's eyes shot a hundred arrows of disgust at the servant but quickly called each of them back, stacked them on a low flame of mortification and let them burn.

Before Jesup could offer his assistance, Spencer slid to the other side of the bed and wormed his way into the wheelchair. His silence formed the order for Jesup to clean up the spilled lunch tray as he pressed a button on the arm of the chair and steered himself out onto the bedroom balcony.

What he needed was pure undiluted sunlight, oceans and oceans of it to bathe each of his cells, to wash his thoughts and memories and blood, to create for him an entirely new existence. He licked his lips at the thought that his desire was more than a fanciful piece of poetry.

As he looked out over the greenery of his estate, the pink

and white blooming dogwoods, lavender azaleas and beds of green-white cabbage flowers, a suffusion of bird songs reminded him that he was still alive. There was still time to fight and it just could be --it just could be--that a new miraculous weapon had been added to his arsenal without his knowing it. His gaze fell on the lush white blossoms of the magnolia tree directly beside the balcony. A smile struggled to pry his lips apart but he fought the urge lest it should prove premature.

He breathed in the gentle syrupy aroma of the tree, the fragrance filling his head like the milk-white light of a blessing. Since the tree had been planted twenty years before, it had sprouted from time to time a new branch or cluster of leaves but had not once blossomed. It had been planted as an anniversary present to his wife, the same year that one of them had given the other that slight discomfort, the souvenir of a summer spent too carelessly. Until a few days ago it had been his intention to have the thing removed, believing it possibly harbored those disgusting shadows that invaded his room. The blossoms, however, did away with that particular theory. Was it just a fluke or had the walls of his jail cracked at last? He had yet to meet the man responsible for the tree's resurrection of life and beauty.

Turning in his chair, he called out to Jesup, "Is the new man still on staff? The gardener. I never see him working."

Jesup, holding the silver tray in one thick hand, walked over to the open glass doors. "He says he prefers to work at night sir. As yet, I've found no reason to refuse that request."

"I see, I see. And he has said nothing to you about how he got Amy's magnolia to bloom? Nothing about his, er, methods?"

"No sir, but I must say he is a lot more effective than the last man. The pink and yellow roses along the front gates have never looked more vibrant, more alive with color."

"More 'alive' you say? And where will he be working tonight?"

"Somewhere near the house sir. Following your instructions, I had him first tend to the borders of the estate then to those areas immediately surrounding the house."

With Jesup's departure, the smile that had been struggling to escape suddenly burst upon Spencer's face as wide and glowing as the blossoms below him. He covered his mouth as he tried to slow the beating of his heart.

Hewman Thorndeaux woke up crying and coughing. He had been dreaming a dream which was more than a dream. In it, he'd seen an old-- No! He didn't want to remember what he'd seen. He quickly focused his attention on his physical surroundings, squeezing the couch on which he'd been sleeping, groping with his vision at the tiny square dining table, the radio on the table, the chair, hotplate and refrigerator. Where was he, what city, state, jail, year, month? Memory came to him slowly, pushing to the back of his skull the tattered remains of his dream. He was working for a rich man, taking care of his plants while living in this little two-room toy house, not far from the larger real house. He recalled several times hearing someone scream during the night and the compulsion to go to him had almost overwhelmed him but the screams had never lasted very long.

Light in the cottage was growing dim. When he looked out the window, he saw that the sun had already crawled below the horizon. The purple-grey sky informed him that it was almost time to start working. He picked up the gin bottle on the floor, held it to his mouth and cursed the dryness that scratched his lips. It was just as well. Better in fact. The alcohol was best when he used it to sleep; while awake, it could prove more treacherous than unexpected lust for an anonymous body.

Three hours later, he was on the east side of the real house running his hands along the heavy withered-looking vines of wisteria intertwined with a huge lattice of wood shaped like a Spanish fan. Back and forth he walked along the vines, softly whispering, softly weeping, softly floating within the solitary bubble of his flesh.

From the curtained windows of a study, Spencer stared at the tall man pacing back and forth before the vines. He could not see the tiny flickers of light sparkling up and down the vines, nor could he see the shimmering sheet of radiance wrapped about Hewman's body, but what he could do was feel the hum and flow of a soft alluring spectacular energy.

The bright lights of Spencer's room did not astound Hewman so much as the figure of the old man himself. Physically, he was not very different from others his age. The wide shoulders indicated he had probably been a large man before the muscles went soft and the green eyes still framed a powerful will but one made less threatening by the nervous twitch leaping from one eye to the other. Spencer dismissed Jesup while Hewman stood wondering why the old man had sent for him.

Yes, thought Spencer, he had heard it was possible --even likely, in fact-- for certain gifts to reside in the forms of those who appeared utterly without value, even as an oyster could be taken for one more crusted seashell if not for the pearl known to rest within.

"Good evening Mr. Thorndeaux. Would you, perhaps, care for a drink?"

Spencer lifted a crystal decanter of brandy from the table beside the bed. The sight of the amber liquid caused a twitch in the lining of Hewman's mouth. Weakness whined at him to take the liquor but instinct shouted to ignore weakness.

"Thank you...but I still got half the night to work."

"Yes yes, of course, of course. I should have realized that a man as skilled as yourself didn't develop such, er, expertise, by drinking on the job. But tell me, where did you learn such mastery over your, ah, craft?"

Hewman shrugged his shoulders and answered, "My father was a farmer. Taught me a lot. Guess I got it from--"

"Talent such as yours is not learned by shoveling shit out of barns Mr. Thorndeaux. Please, you can trust me. Tell me everything!"

A tender prickling rushed beneath Hewman's skin, squeezed past the pores and danced across the surface. What did this old man know about him? Nothing, nothing, how could he know anything?

"Sir, I don't think I know what you mean. If you don't mind, I really ought to get back to work."

"Mr. Thorndeaux, I am eightyseven years old!"

The force and exasperation with which he made this announcement caused Hewman to reverse his turn towards the door. "Men of Holliman blood have rarely lived beyond the age of seventy and I am the only one to have lived this long because I have dared to fight for my life. Using every means available I have waged against death a war as determined and hellish as history has ever seen. Only now I feel a very crucial battle slipping from my grasp and I am in need of assistance, assistance which you can provide."

"I'm not a doctor or a soldier Mr. Holliman."

"No, you're something far more precious than either, a clip from an angel's wing perhaps, a lama returned to flesh as a negro, or a lodestone of white magic wrapped in black human skin."

"Sir you're talking cra-"

The swift rush of an entire wall sliding and disappearing inside another wall made Hewman's head jerk to the right. Turning, he saw the last few feet of the east wall vanish into the floor, revealing a construction of wooden shelves and compartments containing hundreds of books, stacks of magazines, Chinese and African and Mexican figurines, huge pieces of colored rocks and jars holding floating globs in clouded liquid. He stared nearly mesmerized until he heard Spencer yelp and saw him shining a flashlight over the glittering contents on his night table.

The lines of terror slowly dropped from Spencer's face. He hesitated, clicked off the flashlight, then looked at Hewman and said, "I thought I saw one. There on the table...reaching at me from under that...tray."

The look of amazement Hewman trained upon him did not penetrate the sheen of horror covering Spencer's eyes. Finally a flicker of sanity, a glint of calm and focus swam back into his gaze and he spoke, gesturing like a Shakespearean actor towards the wall of objects. He called the odd collection his arsenal and said he had begun putting it together after his only brother had died. His brother, he said, had tried to fight death by purchasing a chain of health food stores along with the minds that ran them, by jogging every day and living in the most agreeable climates throughout the year. But none of that had stopped death from dragging him into the grave at the age of fiftynine. It was then that Spencer decided his own battle for survival would have to be fought differently.

"I sought masters of what some might call the occult. Some bargained away their knowledge; others dismissed me with prayers. London, Paris, Cairo, the backwoods of Georgia and Mississippi, South America--I scoured the globe for those charming things known and unknown to sustain life. It was on such an excursion that I, er, lost my wife. She died in Africa after securing those powders there, the pink and grey ones, from a houganiman near Senegal. And in that also I could see Death's perverse pleasure at my suffering: delivering me a sword with his own hand. Taunting me, slapping me, goading me to the battle."

He had become entranced by the turgid flow of his own words, his memories and determination. He leaned wearily to one side of his wheelchair as though in the telling of his struggles he had once more lived through them, exhausting himself in the process. The sound of Hewman's voice helped to pull him back to the present.

"I'm very sorry to hear about your family's misfortunes Mr. Holliman. I know what it's like to lose somebody you love. But if you think I know anything about all this stuff you got here, you're wrong. I'm a gardener. I trim leaves and fertilize roots, that's all."

"You also lie very poorly Mr. Thorndeaux. People like you are not designed for lying. You can help me and you will help me because you are obligated to do so."

"Obligated? By what? By who?"

"By God, Mr. Thorndeaux! By God, Buddha, the Tao, The All That Is, Allah, the Great White Spirit, He Who Sees and Knows All, call him what the hell you will but he has sent you to me for a very definite purpose!"

"So you figure I'm some kind of miracle worker? Some kind of healer just cause I watered some roses? They say stuff like that works if you believe in it. It's all in the mind."

"No, the power is in the soul; the mind is but a dim reflection thereof!"

"Then why don't you use yours? Do whatever you need to for your self."

"Because I am cut off from it damn you! Don't you see!? The greater part of my life has been spent manipulating and cultivating the coarser elements of existence. My mind cannot release its grip on the material. Nor do I dare to close my eyes for very long in order to 'seek within.' And yes, I have stretched forth my hand to absorb the naked substance of vivification but only to draw it back cold and empty. But I have also seen your hands stretch forth and I know that they runneth over as abundantly as David's cup."

Hewman looked from Spencer's pleading eyes to his own thick steady hands, slowly shaking his head. The old man was wrong. It was not him but something near or inside him that chose to affect wonders at times. There came to his mind an image of his Andrena's body, as lifeless as a rag, draped over his arms as he screamed, cried, prayed, cursed and tried to caress the life back into his wife's flesh. All to no avail. The old man was making him remember too much. Devoid of alcohol's numbing armor, he felt himself stripped to the raw and pink surface of his most vulnerable nerves. As he floundered within the tide of his own rising confusing emotions, he sensed a sudden flash of panic within the old man.

"Look, I'm sorry Mr. Holliman but you made a mist-"

"DO NOT DENY ME!"

Spencer slammed both fists down on the arm controls of his wheelchair, causing it to jump forward. An abbreviated scream shot from his throat as he slammed backwards. Instinct erased Hewman's thought to sidestep the missile rushing towards him and he instead grabbed both metal arms, forcing the chair to an abrupt halt. He could not tell if the sudden stop had flung Spencer against him or if he had leapt out of the chair; he knew only that Spencer's arms had fastened themselves about his neck and the length of his body dangled heavily against his, their faces embracing, their chests, hips and knees meshing.

Breathless and reeling from his scare, Spencer whispered hotly, fiercely, "I'll put a million dollars, no, five, five, I'll give you five million dollars if you save me!"

"I can't!" Hewman grabbed at Spencer's wrists to unlock his grip.

"You can! I can feel the power inside you! I can feel it!"

Spencer summoned strength he had not known he still possessed to tighten his grip about Hewman's neck and squirmed feverishly against him, looking much like a peculiar breed of dog trying to mount the wrong end of another peculiar pedigree. With a single powerful pull, no longer mindful of whether or not he hurt Spencer, Hewman broke his hold and shoved him back into the chair. He backed away from him, feeling for the door while keeping his gaze on Spencer.

"You can't keep power like that to yourself! You can't be that cruel! Damnit, I'm worth a billion dollars! I'll give you everything! Every fucking dime!"

Hewman ran from the room and did not stop until he had reached his cottage. He scrambled around the single room, blindly reaching for things until he realized he did not know what he was doing. He fell on his knees with his forearms slamming against the bed mattress. His fists hammered against the bed, he held his head back and a dragon-roar soared up from his lungs, flames of anguish, sparks of hate and a thick smoke of sorrow clouding the cottage.

Was he cursed that he could not find one inch of a corner in which to live his life without fate or a man laying claim to his mind's peace? Cry and I will gouge your eyes out! Try me.

What would he do now? Where would he go? He tried to rise from the floor and a huge boot of weariness came down on his neck. After placing an entire state between him and his last job, how could he have been so careless as to let the old man find out about him? Yet, even as he asked himself this he knew he was not sure what the old man had seen because he was not always consciously aware of when or how those certain energies manifested within himself; he had pretended for too long that they did not exist. Nonetheless, the excuse was a poor one because one thing he had known was that he'd been using minimal manual labor to tend to the estate.

In his mind's eye he saw the face of the little boy in the last town where he'd worked. He had seen a speeding car strike the boy down and immediately ran to lift the child out of the street. The moment their flesh touched, that vast space inside opened as if of its own accord and he felt the lights and vibrations of his inner self mingling, subsidizing, communing with that of the boy's, bathing him in what he called the screaming river of his very singular soul. More than a dozen people had watched the boy wake up in his arms and walk away with only a slight limp. Those who had witnessed the occurrence called Hewman everything from a demon sorcerer to a herald of God. He had fled the town before the moon rose.

He saw himself now on a tree swing, breezing back and forth in the middle of a forest, the stricken boy lying across his lap crying. Each time he swung back, the boy's face would change to Andrena's, the head would lift up and she'd spit in his face. Above them was a huge burning moon shining down on the spit and tears shimmering upon his face. He then heard a sound as though the largest trees in the forest were all falling towards him, one by one, boom boom boom! Hewman suddenly woke up, wiping frantically at his face. He realized he'd been dreaming but still heard the booming sound from his dream. Where was it--the door. It was coming from the door where someone was outside knocking and calling his name.

As he scrambled to his feet, he tried to guess how long he'd been asleep. It was still dark and it took him several seconds to recognize Jesup when he opened the door.

"I need you to come with me, Hewman. Mr. Holliman has taken a turn for the worse and he's been asking to see you."

"I can't help him."

"Of course not. But whatever differences you had with the old man won't matter now. Is it too much for you to humor a

93

dying man his final request? Please go to him while I get Dr. Amis."

Jesup left before Hewman could respond. The smart thing to do would be to run. No, if the old man really did die they might think he'd had something to with it. As he stepped outside the cottage he did not know what he was going to do until he found himself standing in the lighted doorway of Spencer's bedroom. His gaze fell first on the wheelchair turned over by the bed, then on Spencer's long slight form pulling across the carpet, one arm swinging wildly behind him as though fighting off a pack of wild dogs. Spencer looked through the bars of his terror just long enough to see Hewman standing in the door. A pitiful smile trembled behind the pained fear on his face.

"Oh, I knew you would come. I knew you'd come. You see them don't you, the shadow things, yes, yes, I knew God would send you to save me."

Hewman did not see any shadows but he felt within the room a strange cool pressure as though the entire area were being pressed under a giant palm of air. He walked over to Spencer and knelt beside him. Spencer clawed his way partly into Hewman's arms. Hewman placed one huge hand behind the old man's head to steady its wavering.

"I can't save you old man."

"Yes yes you can you can... save me, please, save me..."

He was so hungry for life and Hewman felt so drained of it that he could only cry. He bent his lips to the old man's forehead and as the two warm surfaces touched he heard himself mumbling something, a prayer or poem or something with which he was completely unfamiliar. It seemed to be coming from the depths of a memory somewhere behind those memories which he knew.

"Yes, see, it's coming to you. God is doing it for you. Yes yes."

He felt the old man stirring, then relaxing, a fragile skiff skimming along the waving surface of cadence spilling from his lips.

"Yes Mr. Thorndeaux, you are doing it, I recognize those words. They are from- Wait! Those words! They do not bind souls to the body, they separate--"

His body went suddenly limp in Hewman's arms and a soft hissing rose from the back of his skull, then was silent. The pressure in the room increased even more until Hewman thought it would crush him against the floor when suddenly it dissipated completely. Off in some distance beyond physical boundaries he heard the old man still ranting and raving. Mixing into the sound came a lullaby draped in Andrena's voice. The old man's tirade changed to an expression of surprise, then one of laughter as Andrena's lullaby continued to flow. On his knees in that strange room flooded with the brilliance of a thousand dying stars, Hewman pulled the old man's empty body more fully into his arms, rocking him gently, rocking him slowly.

I Made My Boy Out of Poetry

I made my boy out of poetry. The good sugared womb of a secret
smile from God opened just that once HALLELUJAH! opened
just that once for me. Stars of Horus smiling down over the
Greek dude's shoulder watched my fingers squeeze through
rhymes 'til made my boy out of poetry, spun his hair rain-forest
nappy like the lush rudeness of jazz jacking off in America's face
carved and drumbeat his bones out of my own immaculate
mysteries out of black gold and silver moon out of golden rose
and ebony song out of oceanhot night and riverwild dawn I made
a whole noisy boy --MADE MY BOY-- out of poetry. Cut the
love straight from my stargazed heart, shaped all three of his eyes
from the mud and gospel that flowed like tongues that flowed like
tongues transformed a magician into his phallus each toe and
finger I moulded like Malcolm building himself into a master
teacher like Langston chanting a flawless psalm then I sang my
boy a giant soul OH I SANG MY SON A GIGANTIC SOUL
I slammed my chest and bled pure holy tears blew clear perfect
thunder from two wondrous nostrils and made my boy out of
poetry.

Poets Everywhere and Always
(for Federico Garciá Lorca)

For you who have huddled beneath
cardboard clouds of cheerless midnight,
your heart pulled taut like a fisherman's net
overstuffed with creatures of the good,
with creatures of beauty and of neverfading evil,
in honor of you I step through life
as if through a field of sleeping gods
picking from the garden of their dreamers' bliss
a bouquet of light to color and feed your immortal light.

How long have your words run
like white stallions charged with black lightning
through the desert of my fears and prayers?
And when did the kindness of your voice
seduce and bless the meekness of my voice?
I was born a pilgrim damned by namelessness
and gifted with blindness until you
bathed my heart in a holocaust
of love and a firestorm of vision.

To you who weaned yourself of half-penny passions
and took in your arms the fury of life's glory
and joy's betrayals, who held at your breast
the lips of those starving for your death:

To the shattered heart of Jalaluddin Rumi,
    teaching time how to dance and oceans how to weep;
To the trembling hands of Walt Whitman,
    glowing with America and feverish with courage;
To the mystical passion of Jean Toomer,
    black as Africa and blue as eternity;
To the warrior-woman throat of Gwendolyn Brooks,
    sweet horn of plenty still tumbling walls;
To the unchained soul of Pablo Neruda,
    riding hurricanes over despair's bullshit dictators;
To the JuJu-spirit eyes of James Baldwin
    and the saxophone bones of Billie Holiday;
To the Buddha-child laughter of Jack Kerouac
    and the rose-perfumed miseries of Jean Genet.

To each of you in future hours and present tense
warming the dark with your spiritual naked Self--
worshippers of women and caressers of men,
Beholders of God and guardians of my madness
did I tell you I was born a pilgrim? I was
damned by namelessness and gifted with blindness
until you bathed my heart in a holocaust
of love and a firestorm of vision.

For the Love of the Poet

Your rhymes are rarely
phonetic
but rather you match
images
with meanings and golden-hued possibilities.

I want a life just like that,
where the outside skin of everything
is as sweet and sticky as inside.

Your meter refuses
to restrain itself
runs wild like a herd of psychedelic be-bops
setting fire between the knees
of an otherwise cool Saturday night.

I want to love that way.
Creating a new color for each sky
believing itself a blue limitation.

And your voice (Ahhh that thundering
planet of a voice) your voice
like a magician repairing
shattered imaginations
like a physician unpuzzling the magic
of the absence of love in his touch.

That's how I want to be reborn:
thoroughly reeking with liberation's blood
and glittery with the flames of all naked joy.

Seized By The Perils Of Poetry

Seized by the perils of poetry
surely I am damned and doomed
quite properly to hell,
I am thrown beyond Paradise
and made love to by Eagles.

Seized by the truth and the cock
and the holy ghost scream of poetry
I run through public spaces
as naked as an "I" without
his dot or mascara or lines
to define where he thinks he stands.

I am seduced and bamboozled,
made discombulate by metaphors:
I ride consciousness
like the unicorn of time galloping
between history's thighs
and his dead whore's nonreality,
I am the heat that loved your mouth
when first you tasted fire,
I am curiosity of the eclipse
looking down at Jesus and wrapping his
blood in the earthquake of my blackness.

Seized by the perils of a resurrection gone wild
I have lost count of my colors and genders
kidnapped by a fuck that never stops
my tongue explodes into thorns
and my chest glows geometric with visions,
somewhere to the east of his skull
the moon is loving me full of madness
and we are dancing to everything
that rhymes with this one gorgeous moment,
we are eating our tambourines raw
smoking big fat lions and shooting
long cool breezes with a singer named God.

Once Upon A Time Eternity Lifted A Pen

You are the line no other poet can write,
a precision of human length and depth
that shall refuse to breathe
unless you place your lips upon
your own existence and grant it
the permission of your breath and truth.

Each letter, space and punctuation
comes from a country governed
by the wisdom of your very individual passion
and your distinctly passionate wisdom.
They will neither dance nor glow except that
you sing the sacred fire of everything you are.

You are the lines and stanzas and titles
and the grandly-jeweled universal meanings
which no other heart can communicate.
Once upon a time eternity lifted a pen,
placed it lovingly upon a divine scroll
and wrote the only copy of you there is.

Two Poems & A Funky Red Rhythm
(To Receding Wave: a Christmas card of sorts)

Saturday morning in the woods beside the lake I was
crawling through bushes picking berries and orchids when I
entered a clearing where two poems and a funky red rhythm
took slow tortured measure of each other's heat and magic.

One poem was a finely crafted piece of womanism,
a sonnet luminous like consecutive orgasms dressed in nothing
but the naked wet of some delicious unseen tongue,
her lines flowing in and out of themselves
like tortured bits of love happily eating each other alive.

And the other poem was a totem pole of masculine themes,
a very muscular exercise in throbbing free verse
with odd images that somehow held themselves together,
images like oversized gods weeping on their mothers' breasts,
like little boys & girls blowing bubbles through each others'
      hearts.

And among those three that I saw, the funky red rhythm
was the strangest: a creature translucent and elastic
with arms like molten symphonies and thighs of jazz
crazily magnificent. Its torso and head brilliant
with the music of heaven melting the earth in its arms.

I stood behind a tree and watched as they flowed
toward each other, the two poems and the funky red rhythm.
And seeing them, the things they did, my clothes burned away
and drops of white flame poured from my scalp,
trailed wet fire down my spine and steam across my chest.

Was I insane, moving blindly towards them until they
pressed upon me, one swallowing me as if I were a sword
coated with chocolate, another lashing me with a flurry
of sacred tremors, and the third--twirling my soul like a baton?
I screamed, and I died, and my mind got lost in the flood of its
      tears.

I woke up with several elderly people standing over me,
asking what had happened, and where were my clothes?
"I was trying to write a poem," I wept without shame, "but the
poem seduced my meanings and the words wrote me instead."

102

Poet of the Resistance
(Emmanuel Carnevali 1900-?)

Carnevali, Carnevali,
poet of the resistance
you never could resist
your shameless love for the grave
and your beloved hunger for truth.
Oh Gentle Brother to beauty,
Oh shameless sister to passion
you never did care to resist
that slow blue fate
so common to every angel.

You who loved Rimbaud
could not be saved by him.
You who worshipped Whitman
swallowed his voice deep into your heart
and wove his beard upon your soul
but could not, dear Carnevali, be saved by him.

Death cursed your name
and how happily you pissed in his face.
Seizures terrorized your body
but your mind would not relinquish
the wealth of your clairvoyant love.
A young general too impatient
to avoid the front lines
you ordered us to keep language
intense and alive, to prevent
oppression from carving truth
into a coffin, and poetry into a corpse.

Carnevali, Carnevali,
poet of the resistance
magic-eyed muse to the genuises of your time.
You: who dared to scold Hemmingway and Joyce and Williams.
The shimmer of your spirit still warms horizons
decades beyond the fury of your passage
    resisting the casual chill of obscurity,
     declining the sentimental courtesies of tragedy.

the poet

flesh, as dark as mystery.
supple like palm trees,
formed his only pen.

and his soul, fluid like full
breasts, bottomless like knowing:
his inexhaustible ink.

he treads deserts and rivers,
jungles and alleys, his ragged
feet bleeding flawed haikus
over the tongues of the earth.

A Stardust Philosopher:
Questions & Voices & Shadows of A Doubt

Are you my lover, whose eyes call like burning eagles
out of fields of murmuring white?
It is not your tragedy that takes the shape
of a human being breathing beside me,
but your curiosity towards we, the so-called living,
and our unrelenting lust for self-righteousness.

I am looking to you for intimations
of an afterlife, where once again
I can watch my laughter cascade from your throat
like neon daffodils and tiny transparent secrets.
But you have come for answers to numerous questions:
You want to know about infants dying
from an illness they've had no time to comprehend.
And you shout at me: about the evil
that inspires humanity to spend billions
researching bombs, but barely pennies
to learn how to heal such chilling ignominy.

Is that you, oh father? Or my brother, perhaps?
I recall sharing with you a love without malice or doubt.
Or are you... are you my mother? My child?
Flinging tears from some distant legend
until I am showered with this need
to let my voice become your voice:
You ask how it makes sense
that millions of people applaud two men
hammering each other with gloved barbarity
but claim repulsion at the sight of them
sharing the civility of a private embrace.
"Why are there no charts tracking the ebb
and flow of national psychoneurosis like those
which indicate financial instability
or geological whimsy? Such a device
would make clear the level to which
our inhumanity has risen, and allow shame
to bring it down a notch or two."

Is that you my lover, you my father, you my child,
transformed by apathy into a stardust philosopher?
You ask these questions as if I am personally
responsible for answers that will change this world.
And I begin to think that maybe I am.

The Man That Poetry Made

The man that poetry made stands luminous
on the broken corners of history's suicidal cravings,
he watches splashing in the street
birds cleaning their feathers inside
the crystal flow of words he gave them,

he is a vintage wine now
traveling with ease over the tongues
of other people's intentions,
he is a quilt
made of one billion black hands
spread like guarantees from a single living God
over the heads of the misbegotten.

The man that poetry made wonders
on which day will he finally recite his soul.
Ask him who his mother is
and he will sing for you memories
of bosom-heavy haikus
filling his mouth with the milk and nectar
of joy neverdying.
Ask about his father
and he will boast about a ballad
that thundered all the way
from Spain to Zaire
bouncing him like a sack full of sonnets
upon his broad whistling shoulders.

This man that poetry made stumbles barefoot
through the city, a huge blue ribbon wrapped
around one big toe, a small pink one tied
to the other, ragged jeans loose
upon free-verse hips, fluorescent eyes blinking
surrealistic kisses of negritude revisited--

To the woman confused
by his lust for peace
he begs "forgive me lovely genius
I was not born as you were born,
my blood was written
by a different kind of coupling."

To the man frustrated
by his lack of animalia
he sang, "Beauty is a thing finer
than exalted fears of actual love."

The man that poetry made sometimes
blows himself to pieces with bombs
made from metaphors, he enjoys watching
the words that shape his life
scatter like golden ashes of imagination
then one by one float back down to earth
covering him with forms and meanings
he never knew existed.
People passing the corner
where he stands luminous and throbbing
rarely see a man at all.
They look at the man that poetry made
and see a public toilet
or a burning bush flaming in the most unlikely place.
Sometimes they see him as a rare jewel
and snatch him up before anyone else
can look. He is always curious riding along
inside the pockets of strangers
wondering how they shall react
when they see him for what he is,
and he reveals, with
love lighting up his every cell
exactly who they are.

Angels and Shakespeare

"For this reason Monday burns like
oil... and it howls in passing like a
wounded wheel..."
Pablo Neruda
(Walking Around)

When I woke yesterday morning, I was certain that I was sup-
posed to be dead but the fact is my eyes were open, I could
smell the pale white sunlight flooding the bedroom, an over-
heated melody burned hard between my thighs and guitar
sounds riding on ocean waves floated up from a CD player to
nibble teasingly at my ears.

Maybe there's been a mistake, I thought, then closed my
eyes again and waited for some holy presence to lift me out of
my doubt and flesh and thinking. A number of lights did come
to me and one even sang my name with a soothing seductive
baritone, yet eventually my eyes opened again and stared out
into a room that was both beautifully strange and harshly
familiar.

Slowly, I rose up and sat on the edge of the bed, the sheets
not sticky but definitely moist with the humidity of nocturnal
evolutions. Is this my afterlife, I wondered, and carefully con-
sidered those words: is this MY afterlife, not THE afterlife,
because I'd always had a dread of falling into other people's
versions of hell or heaven. If either of these existed then I
wanted them custom-designed to fit my own specific sins and
good works.

I stood up to test the weight, the bounce and heat and
validity of my body. Perhaps, if I walked slowly away from the
bed, I might look back and discover my physical form resting
stone-like on the mattress and see that the form in which I was

now moving, manipulating sensation and perception, was my new body and reality, a dazzling vehicle constructed from God's good humor and my soul's aching determination to inhabit a brilliant spiritual reality.

At first I tried to will myself to float across the room, utilizing wings of pure energetic thought and nothing else. After concentrating right up to the edge of a massive headache, I walked rapidly to the doorway, the lush beige carpet licking the soles of my feet, and took a slow deep breath. What would I see when I turned around? Would my corpse resemble the physical being I'd always believed myself to be, or would I be shocked by an image of unimaginable hideousness, terrifying beauty, or deadly nondistinction?

I turned around. The bed was empty. Without question, I was probably alive, and this burning revelation made me piss like a horse where I was standing, the sudden cascade of my surprise jolting my feet with acrid warmth and humility.

The belief that I was supposed to be dead had taken root in my consciousness many years before, even before I was a teenager, when I found myself subject not only to a prophetic disposition regarding my mortality but to experiencing any number of signs or indicators supporting the prophecy. My favorite brother (of the four from whom I had to choose) the one who used to offer himself as a decoy for any malice which the world shot in my direction, had been killed when he was fourteen by a policeman who made no excuses for the murder, only citing the fact that Robert Lee, my brother, had been in a neighborhood that was neither black nor his.

My teacher --first grade or kindergarten, I'm not sure now- my teacher responded to the news of my brother's death by sitting me before the entire class and asking me to tell them what I knew about the murder, as casually as if she had asked me to count to ten, or as if she'd inquired whether or not I had remembered to wash my hands after taking a shit. I did accept my chair of blood-smeared honor in front of everyone else and muttered the only words my broken soul could manage: "He, um. .. he was, ... he was my brother..." Yes: my beautiful beautiful dead brother. And I sat before them, staring through their excited faces at honey-colored memories of him, fully aware that he was gone, completely unaware of how his vanished love would track and haunt my life for years and years into the future.

And it must have been about that time as well --the early

to mid-sixties-- that American journalists and sociologists began to chronicle the decline of the black American male. We were suddenly labeled an endangered species as if the previous decades and centuries of lynchings and slavery and quasi-slavery had never resulted in the cumulative actuality of black men's destruction. In the decades to come we would see elaborate chronicles and presentations of these attempts at slow genocide; artists would draw portraits of us with tiny coffins and skulls in our eyes and hair. National magazines would, seemingly, boast headlines declaring we were nearly gone. And it was true that we were busy killing each other, and others were busy killing us all on a fairly regular basis --whether death came through the ignoble agencies of war, domestic violence, drugs, suicide or diseases that cancelled our sexual appetites, we were exiting the planet at a rate noticeably disproportionate to other groups of our fellow human beings.

Moreover, in the case of my individual being, I was prone to political militancy, both outside of my race and within it, a garrulous gadfly in the mode of a Socrates or Patrice Lumumba who loved to buzz about the glories of change and unification, whose too-loud, too discomforting voice, made me highly susceptible to various forms of target practice. Without the decoy of my brother's presence, one solid hit and my endangered ebony male self would become one more hot item for the six o'clock news.

So it was my firm belief that by the time my thirtieth birthday approached, I would be certifiably dead. When I turned thirty and found myself still breathing, I calmly accepted the fateful fact that death would come the next year, or even, possibly, the next day. At some point, I actually stopped anticipating death but unraveled any ongoing sense of connection with life. In other words, I am rarely certain which reality I occupy, or which reality occupies me, and I move about those spaces which compose my time --the places where I work, live and struggle to play-- with much much caution.

Moving with what I hoped was more grace than fear, I walked from the bedroom through the living room, into the kitchen, lightly touching the furniture and walls as if it were all new to me, which it was because my memory had yet to acknowledge that this experience was real. On the kitchen table, a large six-sided coin made of smoke-colored glass, I found seven or eight envelopes which I hoped would provide answers about who I was or wasn't, about the life I was living or not living, about the death I was entering or not entering.

At first I was surprised to notice that the envelopes were addressed to two different people: one named Jeffery J. Lloyd and another named Aberjhani. I assumed that one of these must be me and immediately became concerned that apparently someone else lived in the apartment, someone who was not presently there and whose face I could not recall. Then I saw something odd. Two of the envelopes had both of these names on them, with one name enclosed in parentheses following the other. For a moment, this confused me even more, for I took it to mean that two people, myself and someone other than I, took turns subjecting one another to some cruel masochistic parenthetical existence, each of them (us?) alternately banishing the other to a form of psychic slavery symbolized by the broken handcuffs of parentheses.

This idea, of psychic enslavement, began to stir cyclones up and down the shores of my nerves. I dug through the letters and scattered papers until I came upon a check and a note explaining very clearly --evidently for the benefit of a bank and publisher-- that the people I had thought of as two, were in fact only one. These two people, as I had thought of them, were both me.

The acquisition of the two names, this delicious double identity, forced me to further accept the likelihood that I was not a ghost experiencing spectral hallucinations but a flesh and blood silly-behind man who not only possessed these two identities but apparently several jobs as well. Exactly what my status was on any of these jobs remained unclear. But I eased away from some of my caution and went to the bathroom for a warm soothing shower. The water rushed over me like a convincing display of grace and I allowed the eager sensuality of it to take over my body until the steam turned into a chilled autumn rain.

When I got out, a telephone was ringing and I walked quickly to the bedroom. I stood near the night stand and watched the phone ring over and over again. How wise would it be to answer that thing, in light of the fact that I was clearly stumbling between the speckled dimensions of self-awareness? Surely not too wise at all. Then it stopped ringing. For a moment, the silence blossomed all around me like a garden filled with jasmine and roses and I felt drunk and sober at the same time. Which one of my names, my two or three or infinite selves, could identify best with such a feeling, such a slow-whirling agony and ecstasy?

I then thought I heard laughter or someone singing. Over in the doorway there stood an exquisite emerald-colored angel with wings that pierced the floor and ceiling. The light of it shined all over my nakedness and burned away the water remaining from my shower. I seized the opportunity presented me:

"Am I alive or dead?" I asked the angel.

"Yes."

"Uh, 'yes' what?"

"Yes you are alive, and yes you are dead."

"Oh. Wow. Ok, but um, can you tell me some definite course of action I should be taking, here and now, and who I should be taking it as? Can you restore my full memory so I'll know what to do?"

The angel stood there, or floated there, wrapped up like a radiant moth in the glowing web of a silence that seemed to occupy a dimension beyond the room where I stood.

"Why did you come here if you're not going to help me? Aren't you supposed to be all powerful unconditional love or something like that?"

"Whatever my Creator commands is the sum total of what I am. Consider me as you would a small finger upon the greater hand of divine decision."

This business about being an extension of divine will sounded familiar and although it did not solve my dilemma, standing there coccooned in my nudity and frustration, I decided not to wrestle with the angel, to simply by-pass Jacob's example and get dressed.

Before I could consider what was happening, a flurry of words, thoughts and sensations fell upon me like a blizzard of colored lights whirling rapidly into my brain, and I knew this was the angel's doing, but again, paid it no mind. Once I was fully clothed, I walked through the doorway as if the angel were not there and even though I pretended not to, I savored the exquisite tingling that leaped under my skin and shot thunder through my bones.

On my way back to the kitchen, I passed two more angels. One gave off a hypnotic aroma, like blossoms weaned on the waters of the Nile, and the other surprised me by humming a fusion of classic melodies by Duke Ellington and Mozart.

I went back to the table where the letters were and read several of them. The emotional tone and rhythm of those addressed to one name was acutely distinct from that addressed to the other; I chose to identify with the name that generated the fatter mounds of kindness.

As soon as I made this decision, the flood of lights and voices came tumbling back into my head. Entire islands and groves of memory suddenly sprung up and I found myself face to face with a deeper awareness of what I can only describe as numerous versions of my singular self and my solitary destiny, pencil sketches of possibilities in which I saw myself as a clown, a poet, a slave, an orator, a prophet and a beggar and a healer and a warrior. I wet my lips and unexpectedly tasted a sweeter deeper sense of knowledge regarding my life.

I did not dwell long upon this shadowy vision. I picked up a briefcase, left the apartment and walked out to the parking lot. I saw a stunning blue full-sized Thunderbird and started to reach for the door handle when the car spoke up and said: "Please do not touch me unless your name is Ardell and you are my owner." My hand froze in a gesture made perfect for tragedy. I realized that I did not, in fact, own a car, and that I needed to hurry if I was going to catch my regular bus at the stop two blocks away.

The bus was pulling up just as I arrived at the stop and I took a seat near the driver, a dark-skinned woman wearing Cleopatra braids. She was friendly and spoke to me as if we knew each other, as if this had been a year when we were lovers then drifted successfully, or not-so-much-so, out of each other's life. She reached back to hand me a clipped newspaper article about a minister who had robbed two motels.

"Can you believe that?!" she said, then went on without waiting for me to tell her I could. "That's the same man who preached in my church Sunday morning --Sunday morning Lord!-- then turned around and robbed Superion Motel that same night! Brother you should'a heard him preach! He had me clappin' happy hands and cryin' happy tears about the days of rapture soon to come. He put so much excitement in my soul that for a while I thought he was Jesus standin' up there in disguise. When he told me I was a chosen servant of God, I was ready to work miracles all over that man --you hear what I'm sayin' brother?-- then he go and rob somebody! A goddamned preacher!"

I looked at the newspaper article then returned it. There were tears on the bus driver's lovely face and tears in her beautiful voice, but the stout blond man sitting across from me was laughing. Loudly. I imagined that the criminal preacher, or the preaching criminal, must be like these two people, one side of him crying over his spiritual failures while the other side laughed at other people's spiritual naiveté.

Fortunately, a few minutes later, the bus stopped right in front of the huge bookstore, more the size of a grocery store, where I worked, and I arrived there ten minutes prior to the start of my shift. The main reason I knew this was because someone smiled and commented on it when I entered the store.

There was a long customer service counter towards the back of the store and I stopped there when I noticed two tall stacks of William Shakespeare's complete sonnets sitting next to a computer. I asked the young woman working behind the counter what the books were for. Her eyes bulged as if she were suffering a sudden massive attack of gas in the brain and she placed both hands on her hips:

"Now you look here Mr. Aberjhani! Just cause you a manager in this store don't mean you got the right to come fuckin' with me first thing in the morning! I'm a human being just like you is and I don't have to take abuse off nobody! So if you wanna fire me then you just go right ahead cause I was lookin' for a job when I found this one goddamnit!"

Her lips trembled to a halt and at that moment I remembered who she was. I recalled as well that brutal language was sometimes her way of singing poetry and sometimes the weapon she employed to wound herself in front of witnesses. I had often wondered, as I did now, about the nature of her beauty, what it must be like when it was not gushing blood out of the rocks of her private damnation.

"Is today Monday?" I asked her.

"It sure is," she answered, her voice loaded with enough attitude to sink a battleship.

"I kind'a thought it was Monday cause it's got that difficult feeling to it. You look very lovely today."

"Thank youuuu..."

I picked up a copy of Shakespeare's complete sonnets, a slim handsome edition done in classic black leather binding, and I thought about the theory that Shakespeare may have been an angel pretending to be human. As I admired the gold lettering on the cover, a woman came walking down the side aisle, followed by a four- or five-year-old child who was screaming as if he had just fallen from her womb and experienced the most cruel awakening imaginable. I opened the sonnets and looked, foolishly I know, for something to read to the child, hoping for words that were soft and truthful to tell his tears, or perhaps for some gentle fable, about how exquisite it can be just to know that one is truly alive.

~ much peace, many blessings ~